ALTERED

BOOK ONE

A Dark Femme Fatale Series

By Aria Paige

EXCLUSIVE
AUDIOBOOK OFFER

VISIT ARIAPAIGE.COM

Get the first 10 chapters of Altered: Book One when you
SIGN UP to Aria Paige's VIP mailing list.

Contents

Act I: The Dispensation of Cora Bishop

Chapter 1: Moth to a Flame   2

Chapter 2: Torn Asunder   7

Chapter 3: Unyielding Inferno   13

Chapter 4: Ethics of Desperation   18

Chapter 5: Uncharted Serum   23

Chapter 6: The Wet Passage Home   30

Chapter 7: An Ominous Revelation   36

Chapter 8: A Detective's Gaze   40

Chapter 9: The Awakening   47

Chapter 10: A Web of Lies   53

Act II: The Dispensation of Lila Thompson

Chapter 11 Devil's Masquerade   61

Chapter 12 Rhea's Arrival   69

Chapter 13: The Masks We Wear   73

Chapter 14: Belly of the Beast Part 1   79

Chapter 14: Belly of the Beast Part 2   83

Chapter 15: Enemy of My Enemy   85

Chapter 16: Between Hell and a Hard Place	92
Chapter 17: Unleashed	98
Chapter 18: A Royal Invitation	104
Chapter 19: Hostile Takeover	112
Chapter 20: Fractured Alliance	121
Chapter 21: The Mad Prince	127

Act III: The Dispensation of Rhea

Chapter 22: Ravaged Part 1	136
Chapter 22: Ravaged Part 2	144
Chapter 23: In His Wake	151
Chapter 24: Rhea's Declaration	160
Chapter 25: Revelations	162
Chapter 26: The Reckoning	167
Chapter 27: A Dark Path	172
Chapter 28: A Beautiful Death	179
Chapter 29 Altered Psyche	188

Final Act: The Dispensation of LILA

Chapter 30: A Pilgrim's Riddle	192
Chapter 31: A Diabolical Conspiracy	200
Epilogue	211

Act I

The Dispensation of

Cora Bishop

Chapter 1
Moth to a Flame

Sam's head tilted, her eyes sparkling with that same mischievous glint that had led us into countless adventures. "Dare I ask, how goes the battle in the trenches of Silicon Valley?"

I shrugged, glancing around the café that had become our haven amid the city's unending bustle. "Hardly the thrill of your journalistic adventures, babe," I smirked, tucking my rebellious auburn curls behind an ear.

"What? All those ones and zeros? There's got to be a scandal buried in there somewhere, Cora!"

"Nope, just chasing ghosts in our new AI blockchain—ouch," I winced as the coffee scalded my tongue. My lips puckered, blowing out cool breaths in an almost comical attempt to soothe the sting.

"Aww, babe, again? You OK?" she said, her expression softening with concern.

Pivoting in her chair, she gestured with her hand. "Excuse me... I demand to speak to the manager immediately—this is unacceptable!" Sam's voice soared in mock outrage, as she fought back laughter.

"Babe, I swear, if you don't stop doing that—Jenn's going to ban us," I half-whispered, trying to resist Sam's infectious humor.

"Yep," came a voice from behind the counter, barely audible above the grind of coffee beans and the hiss of the milk steamer.

I chuckled and continued, "Now my boss has me trying to implement some fancy interface—I'm not even sure it's possible. Apparently, I'm 'helping to shape the future,' he said. I told him if he wants to help shape my future, give me a raise and a promotion, dammit!" Sam laughed, and I winked.

"Any upcoming exposés you can't tell me about?" I asked.

"Erm, nothing noteworthy, as usual—bad guys doing bad things," Sam replied.

"I don't know how you do it, babe, you're the one who needs a raise."

"I wish! My boss acts like he's doing me a favor just paying me every month," she said, allowing a brief laugh to escape her lips.

Our attention was momentarily diverted to Jenn, our waitress on the other side of the café, successfully balancing a stack of cups and saucers to clear a table. We shared a quiet nod of approval.

"She's a real octopus, that one," Sam noted, her attention lingering on the spectacle.

Yet, her eyes were distant, clouded by unvoiced concerns—I could always tell. My arms stretched across the table; fingers tightening around her cold hands. "You know I worry, right? Your work isn't exactly a walk in the park."

Sam smiled. "Isn't it my job to look out for you? Anyway, who wants to talk about that depressing stuff?"

"OK! 'Need-to-know basis' and all that." I relaxed my grip. "So, what else is new? Any interns striving to be the next 'Samantha Webb' bastion of truth?"

"Actually, yes. We've got a new guy, fresh from Columbia University."

"Cool, sounds promising."

"Promising and eager to a fault. Thinks he can solve corruption by simply exposing it."

I laughed. "Ah, youthful zeal, quashed by the unforgiving boot of experience."

"Exactly! Makes me feel ancient. Speaking of which, remember that road trip we took to Pueblo ruins near the Grand Canyon?—we're due another road trip baby!" she proclaimed with an expectant grin.

"How could I forget? You drove us off a cliff, Sam."

"Hey, …added excitement."

"Excitement or a near-death experience?"

"Sam-antics! Ha, see what I did there?"

"Yeah… wow—and I thought my jokes were corny," I shook my head, but she had me. We both burst out laughing—the earlier tension replaced by shared memories and lighter moments. We lingered for a while, letting the aroma of coffee and companionship surround us like a warm blanket.

As we rose to leave, the café door chimed in farewell. "Travel safe, girls," Jenn smiled as she maneuvered past, performing yet another impossible balancing act.

Outside, the sun had begun to paint the sky with hues of pink and orange when Sam broached the subject. "Cora, I'm thinking of visiting my dad's grave next week."

Her announcement draped a shroud of silence over us, holding back the parting words that had been on the tip of our tongues.

"I'll come with you," I replied, hoping to offer solace.

"I love you, babe," Sam said.

"You better," I replied, rubbing her shoulders.

She leaned in with a warm hug as we bid farewell.

"Take care. Call me," I said, projecting my voice.

She smiled and blew a kiss as her silhouette merged with the bustling crowd. But still, a sense of foreboding lingered. Her stories regularly delved into murky waters, unearthing unsettling truths that most preferred to stay buried. Despite her promises to tread lightly, I could not dispel my fears. She was an unerring moth drawn to the flame of truth, even if it risked her well-being. Yet, I found strength in knowing she was a fighter, a survivor who had navigated numerous trials with a stoic resolve.

My thoughts drifted back to her Arizona upbringing—rugged and authentic, shaped by harsh desert terrain. Her hair, once a rich chestnut brown, had lightened over the years to a windswept blonde, bleached by hours spent exploring the Saguaro landscape, not far from her childhood home.

Abandoned from a young age, she faced difficulties and abuse as she cycled through a series of foster homes, each one less nurturing than the last. At 13, she struck out alone, surviving months on the streets through sheer grit and determination. These hardships fostered a powerful spirit of independence and a deep empathy for the disadvantaged.

But then she met Peter and Amanda Webb, who became the loving adoptive parents she had always craved. Their patient kindness started the gradual process of healing the emotional wounds from her childhood. Around this time, the Webbs moved to California for Peter's work.

I remember that first day of 10th grade when Sam walked into our classroom, scanning the unfamiliar faces. As our eyes connected, it was like two long-lost sisters recognizing one another. From that moment on, we were inseparable.

However, Peter's death from a violent assault 3 years ago left a significant void in her world. He had been a strong, fatherly figure, and Sam had come to appreciate his grounding influence. Amanda, her adopted mother, remained a maternal presence, but with Peter now absent, the relationship became more distant in their shared grief. The drive to find purpose fueled Sam, motivated by a desire to rectify life's cruelties.

Once she found her calling as a journalist, her unwavering quest for justice had been a constant source of worry for me. What was this new, heinous story she was pursuing? A tale of political subterfuge? A scandal concealed within corporate walls? Or worse?

Yet, Sam had always protected me—whether it was from bullies at school or dealing with a jerk boyfriend. Despite our shared age, she possessed a warm maternal instinct that I cherished. And without a family of my own, she was all I had. Regardless of the challenges she faced, there was nothing I wouldn't do to help her. And that was not about to change.

Chapter 2
Torn Asunder

The sun streamed through the window blinds, casting dust-filled stripes across my screen. I glanced at the clock; it was 2 P.M., that typical Tuesday lull where the excitement of the morning hustle had already faded into routine.

My workstation was cluttered yet functional—minimalist chaos reflecting the grind of a tech analyst. I sat, clicking through spreadsheets, evaluating algorithms, and responding to work emails that ranged from urgent to trivial. In the background, my playlist churned out a steady beat of Lo-Fi tunes, a subtle backdrop to my focus. A sip of lukewarm coffee momentarily lifted me from autopilot mode, which would usually set in around this time of day.

I leaned back in my chair, interlocking my fingers behind my head. I decided to seize a moment of reprieve before diving back into the tasks that awaited me. Time seemed both to drag and race, a strange paradox. Just as I was about to turn my attention to a challenging problem, my phone broke the familiar pattern of the afternoon.

The screen lit up. That had to be Sam—she was the only one who called me from an unknown number. I expected a casual chat, perhaps a quick follow-up from the night before, or maybe an amusing exchange of memes—We often did that to break the monotony of the day. With a half-smile, I picked up the phone, swiped to answer, and held it to my ear.

"Hey girl, miss me?" I asked.

There was a brief pause. The voice that greeted me was decidedly not Sam's. It was male, gravelly, and carried a note of solemnity.

"Is this Ms. Cora Bishop?" he asked.

"Yes. Who's calling, please?" I responded, my tone betraying the surge of unease.

"I'm Detective Mack with the San Jose Police Department. Do you know a 'Ms. Samantha Webb'?"

"Yes, she's my best friend. Is there a problem?" I asked, trying to maintain my composure.

"Are you familiar with Route 101, the north-south highway near Gilroy?"

"Yes, of course. Detective, what's going on?"

"I'm afraid Ms. Webb has been involved in a collision."

"What do you mean, a 'collision'? A car accident?"

"I'm afraid so Ms. Bishop."

"When? Is she okay? Where is she?" I stammered.

"She lost control of the vehicle—swerved into oncoming traffic." His voice was steady, a cold contrast to my emotional disarray.

"I'm afraid she didn't survive. The authorities ruled it an accident."

His condolences sounded empty, and his regret mechanical.

"What? That's impossible. She can't be."

The Detective explained further. "From what we can tell, she lost control and struggled to keep the car on the road. Look, Ms. Bishop…"

The phone clattered to the floor, the detective's voice cutting out as the room began to spin. I staggered, my knees sapped of strength. I was in complete shock, my soul hollowed by confusion and disorientation. Sam was invincible, a force of nature. How could she be gone? He must have been mistaken. My fingers instinctively clung to the pendant around my neck as I tried to make sense of what I'd just been told. This could not be happening.

A profound ache seized my stomach, the shock constricting like a vice. I lurched, grappling for support that wasn't there. Sounds foreign and guttural erupted. The rawness of grief laid bare in each wail that ripped from my throat. I swayed, as my breaths became short and ragged, a counterpoint to the pulsing in my ears. Collapsed against the wall, every heave of my chest was ladened, and every cry that escaped me felt like an unbearable loss.

Sleep eluded me that night. I lay in bed, wrestling with the detective's unsettling words as the sentence replayed over and over: "...a collision. I'm afraid she didn't survive."

My eyes kept checking the phone, yearning to see a missed call or a message from Sam—anything that would disprove this terrible nightmare. Failing to silence my thoughts, I greeted the dawn with a heavy heart—I had to identify Sam's body.

***

Later that afternoon, I walked into a sterile room, my shoes making a faint squeaking sound against the linoleum floor. The walls were an unassuming shade of beige, as if trying not to draw attention to themselves. The fluorescent lights hummed quietly above, casting a harsh, unforgiving glare on the steel gurney that held Sam's body draped in a white sheet.

A middle-aged woman in scrubs and a lab coat approached me, clipboard in hand. Her expression was professional, but devoid of warmth. "Ms. Bishop, I'm Nurse Anderson. Are you ready?"

"Can you ever be ready for something like this?" My voice barely rose above a whisper.

"I suppose not," she answered softly, before pulling back the sheet.

I froze, dreading the moment. But there Sam was, her face almost peaceful, yet noticeably drained of the vivacious energy that had defined her.

She broke the heavy silence. "Is this Ms. Samantha Webb?"

My heart sank. "Yes," I admitted, although every ounce of my being wished it was a lie.

"We need a formal identification for our records. Sign here, please." She extended the clipboard and a pen toward me.

I scrawled my signature almost without looking, finalizing the reality in ink. It was irrevocable now, captured in the neat lines of a bureaucratic form. Nurse Anderson moved to cover Sam's body again. "Is there anything else you need, Ms. Bishop?"

I looked at Sam one last time; her face now just a mask of what she once was. "No."

She nodded. "The funeral home will be here shortly for the transfer. You should say your goodbyes."

I touched the pendant around my neck one more time as I looked at Sam, my best friend, my sister, now rendered silent forever. The cruel irony was that she had always been the brave one. Now, it was me who had to find the courage to face a world without her.

As I left the room, she replaced the sheet over Sam's body, her movements methodical and practiced. Her eyes met mine for a brief moment, offering a glance of sympathy before turning away. The door closed behind me with a soft click, sealing a part of my life I would never recover.

***

Days melded into nights, punctuated by unimaginable pain. Her absence felt like a phantom limb, a perpetual reminder of a bond severed too soon. My world seemed to shrink. The color drained, and the music muted. All that remained was a shell, echoing with the emptiness that now consumed me. I oscillated between moments of paralyzing grief and fleeting denial, convinced it was a cruel prank. I hoped any second now, Sam would waltz through the door, her face lit with that infectious, unabashed grin.

Her funeral was a monochromatic blur of condolences and whispered reminiscences. Amanda, her stepmother, and I attempted to console each other. Yet, I felt truly alone, an island amidst the crowd, holding on to the void that our once-loving friendship had become.

In the passing days and weeks, Sam's death loomed larger, the weight of her absence pulling me under whenever I tried to emerge. With her gone, a part of me seemed to vanish as well.

Back at Sam's apartment, her desk, usually littered with a mix of scattered notes and disposable coffee cups, sat untouched. Haunted by memories of our laughter, her determination, and her unwavering spirit. I found myself alone, adrift at sea, sinking deeper into depression and hopelessness.

Yet, amid the fog of sorrow, something was amiss. It was an unsettling feeling that wouldn't dissipate. Sam was careful, meticulous even; the circumstances of her "accident" began to seem increasingly incongruent with the person I knew—especially considering our last conversation. The more I turned it over in my mind, the less the story aligned. Something about the police reports, the details of the collision, and the coroner's ruling—it all refused to add up. Sam was too experienced a driver to make such a fatal error. This was a girl who grew up racing souped-up vintage cars on the dusty back roads of Arizona. She wouldn't simply lose control driving down a damn highway.

That sensation in my gut intensified, coalescing into a suspicion that became increasingly hard to ignore. But was I fabricating scenarios to avoid the finality of her death? Or was I onto something no one else cared to notice? In the midst of doubts and mysteries, one clear purpose anchored me—I would uncover the truth no matter the path I had to tread.

Chapter 3
Unyielding Inferno

I stared out the window of my apartment, watching the city hum on this rain-soaked morning, hardly bothering to register the day. A mug of herbal tea sat cooling on the table beside me, the floral scent barely noticeable anymore. Sam bought me that mug—she always noticed the little details.

I replayed our last conversation—while her face appeared composed; I knew something was wrong. She would become distant and lost in her thoughts, but would always try to shield me from the dangers she faced.

It became apparent that her fleeting expression hinted at a secret more disconcerting. What if she had discovered a story so troubling that it made her a target? Sam had a knack for ruffling feathers with her uncompromising journalism. What if someone wanted her silenced?

I kept recalling—her pen-nibbling habit deep in thought, her thrill over discovering a new lead, and her commitment to exposing the truth. I sighed, the familiar ache of missing her resurfacing. It had been weeks since her tragic death, but it still didn't seem real that she was gone. I felt helpless, not knowing where to turn, or who to ask.

"What would Sam do?" I wondered.

Confused and frustrated, I picked up the phone and started making calls. First, I dialed the police, my voice filled with repressed urgency, fishing for anything that might serve as a clue.

Their stonewalling answers, wrapped in bureaucratic nonsense, were anything but helpful.

Next, I called Sam's circle—friends, acquaintances, colleagues, and even her intern. Each conversation veered from small talk to insinuations, with probing questions never zeroing in on the truth.

"I'm just trying to piece together the last few weeks of her life," I'd say. Nevertheless, no one was willing to untangle the knot for me—something was off. Time became elusive as nights blurred into days during my feverish "investigation." I pinned notes and stickies to my corkboard, which served as a make-shift HQ for all my research. I scoured her blog, combing through old stories in search of leads. I dug through her social media contacts, cross-referencing names with the days leading up to her death, seeking an unusual pattern or connection.

In the early hours of the morning, exhausted and slouched over my desk, I couldn't escape the fact that I was getting nowhere. Then, as I sat staring down multiple dead ends, a bolt of realization struck me. How could I have overlooked it? Sam's laptop! Her notes, writings, investigations, contacts—the last story she was working on, there had to be something.

My hands scrambled for a sweater and jeans that lay in a pile of unwashed clothes as I headed for the door. If Sam had left breadcrumbs, I needed to find them and follow wherever they led.

Fueled by a renewed sense of focus, I drove toward her home as the car's engine revved in unison with my thoughts. Each stoplight was an unwelcome pause, ratcheting up my frustration. I navigated empty streets, passing boarded-up shops, their abandoned state reflecting my growing unease.

Eventually, I pulled onto her road, my tires meeting her gravel driveway with a quiet screech. Breathing deeply to calm my nerves, I let myself in with the spare key and switched on the hallway lamp. The room flickered into view as Sam's laptop rested on the coffee table, barely visible beneath a haphazard stack of old newspapers and take-a-way cartons.

Her worn but comfortable sofa offered unspoken support as I began the arduous task of combing through her hard drive. It was slow going at first, trying to make sense of her intricate filing system. Gradually, I started piecing together names, dates, and connections. She had been digging deep as usual, uncovering corruption that powerful people wanted hidden—bribery, election rigging, insider trading, but nothing stood out of the ordinary.

The sun was already peeking above the horizon by the time I came across an encrypted file labeled "R." This had to be important. I could feel Sam urging me on as I dove into cracking the encryption. I perched myself on the edge of the couch as lines of code went to work. Exhausted after hours of watching the screen, I had dozed off, but I was soon awoken by the laptop's notification. My eyes struggled to adjust. Finally, it had paid off: the file stared back at me, now unlocked.

My pulse quickened as I opened the folder, wondering what revelations awaited. The first documents appeared to be financial - endless rows of transactions, offshore accounts, and shell companies. Scanning the lists, I recognized prominent names of politicians interspersed throughout, linked to all manner of illicit activity.

In another folder, I found audio recordings of what sounded like a shadowy tribunal, deciding the fate of someone who had apparently crossed them. "He's become a liability. He has to go," a distorted voice said.

Deep within a string of files, I unearthed encrypted communications between another set of unidentified male voices. Their language was veiled, but amidst the secrecy, the clue I had been searching for finally revealed itself. "Get me that journalist!" My heart stopped, and I felt sick to my stomach. They must have been talking about Sam, and she would have known.

Venturing deeper, I discovered a file detailing illegal activities and conspiracies revealed within a litany of redacted government records, articles, and obscure reports. Everything from murder and kidnappings to extortion, blackmail, and bribery.

Suddenly, two words, scattered throughout one of the documents, leaped off the page - "THE RING." Now, the 'R' made sense, but it only deepened the mystery. What was this sinister organization? Government? Criminal? Both? What had she uncovered? And if they were indeed responsible for her death, why were the police covering it up?

I fell back, sinking into Sam's couch, stunned by the magnitude of her discoveries. She must have known the danger she was in, and yet instead of turning to me for help, she protected me, as usual.

I should have seen the signs and realized how much trouble she was in. My best friend had entered the lion's den, and I had been oblivious. I rubbed my eyes and exhaled a mix of anger, sorrow, and guilt. Sam had sacrificed her life to expose the truth and paid the ultimate price.

As I sat there, still absorbing the weight of Sam's buried secrets, I felt my focus narrow to a point. Her death was no accident—she had been cruelly and deliberately murdered. Surely, with all this damning evidence, that detective would have no choice but to reopen the case. If there was ever a moment to act, it was now.

Something in my gut tightened. Whether it was a sense of urgency or dread, I couldn't tell. I stood up, fingers already reaching for my phone to make the calls that could no longer wait.

An odd sensation came over me, and the flow of time seemed to slow. A pressure mounted in my head as if it might burst. The room had become suffocatingly hot. Suddenly, my world dissolved into ear-piercing chaos and blistering heat. A concussive force slammed into me, obliterating my thoughts. My body reacted with primal instinct before my mind could comprehend. I was weightless, hurled through the air by a destructive energy.

I gasped for breath, but my lungs filled with ashes lining my insides. Searing pain engulfed every nerve. Time was suspended as the atmosphere became disorientingly thick. A noxious cocktail of smoke and ash replaced oxygen, life's most basic offering, compounding the agony.

Sam's sanctuary, which once offered fleeting moments of peace, transformed into ground zero of a devastating explosion. Then I blacked out, and everything went dark.

Chapter 4
Ethics of Desperation

I shot awake, my vision struggling to adjust to the sterile brightness of the room. Machines beeped and tubes crisscrossed my body, amplifying my feeling of constriction. A ventilator aided my breathing, each inhalation a wisp of mechanical salvation.

My skin was a congealed patchwork of pain. Charred, tenderized, and swollen, it was a physical record of that horrifying moment.

"Where—?" I choked out.

A white-coated figure rushed toward me, a blur in my unfocused vision. "Easy now. You're in the hospital. Try not to move," said a voice.

"I have to leave!" I said, attempting to disentangle myself from the web of medical paraphernalia.

"Explosion. There was an explosion!"

"Hold her!" another voice said.

Two more figures darted in, pressing down on my arms and legs.

"Sam's gone! Murdered! I need her laptop. I need to get to her laptop!"

My thoughts spilled out in frantic bursts, laced with desperation.

"We have to calm her down. Prepare for sedation."

"No!" I thrashed, their faces blurring as my emotions spiraled. "You don't understand. The laptop, it's—"

The needle pierced my arm, and almost instantly, heavy darkness fell over me, swallowing my protests.

I faded in and out of consciousness, catching fragments of hushed conversations between doctors and nurses. Speech swirled around me—"third-degree burns, smoke inhalation, internal injuries." The full gravity of it all remained murky, obscured by morphine.

Lying motionless in the hospital bed, I struggled to process everything that had happened. The deafening explosion, the agonizing pain, losing Sam. My mind reeled from the trauma as my broken body languished, suspended between life and death.

When lucid moments arose, panic would seize me as I remembered the encrypted files, "The Ring," and Sam's unfinished work. I had to pursue it, to unravel the ugly truths that had gotten her killed. But my limbs refused to respond. I was trapped inside this broken shell.

The following two weeks unfolded in a fog of painkillers and frustration. Caught between despair and a restless urge to act, I was acutely aware that my crusade couldn't resume until my body healed. Each tick of the clock felt like a betrayal, knowing that these animals were out there still profiting from their crimes, without a second thought for the lives they've ruined.

My solace came as a singular focus: justice for Sam. This mission consumed my thoughts. In pain and severely incapacitated, the odds were against me, but I still had to find a way out of this hospital. The moment I did, the hunt would resume.

**

After spending what felt like an eternity in the serious burns unit, I regained consciousness. The spectral figure at my bedside, first obscured, morphed into Dr. Evelyn Shore. This intriguing woman seemed to emerge at my darkest moment.

"You're awake, Ms. Bishop," Dr. Shore announced, her voice striking a calculated balance between clinical detachment and genuine concern. "How are you feeling?"

"I need to get out of here," I said, more a rasp than a sentence.

She held my gaze firmly. "Leaving is not an option. You've experienced third-degree burns over a significant portion of your body. You've also incurred severe lung damage from inhaling toxic fumes, not to mention multiple fractures from the blast. Your immediate concern should be your own well-being. Your condition is extremely precarious."

"But you don't get it—" I protested.

"I do," she interrupted, "but you're in no state to act on anything. Your life is what's critical here."

Dr. Shore exhaled deeply, her chest rising and falling in a momentary surrender to her own internal conflict.

"If we do everything by the book—pain management, skin grafts, therapy—you'll be looking at a recovery timeline that stretches out longer than any of us would prefer. Even then, I cannot guarantee you'll regain your full mobility or lung capacity."

Each word she spoke formed a knot in my stomach. "That's not good enough," I said. My words, dry and grating.

The machines beeped in the background, but even they seemed to pause in anticipation. Dr. Shore's expression tightened.

"There's an alternative…" she said, then paused.

"What kind of alternative?" I replied curiously.

"We've been working on a groundbreaking experimental treatment."

"Tell me more," I said, barely more than a whisper.

Dr. Shore moved decisively, pulling a chair close to the bed. The soft scrape of the legs resounded like a drumroll.

"Regenerate skin and potentially erase the horrific scars that now mark your body," she said, locking eyes with me once more. "You could be back on your feet much sooner than traditional methods would allow."

"And the drawbacks?" I enquired.

"Side effects," she replied, the words hanging in the air like a dark cloud. "From minor symptoms to potential complications, we haven't yet fully understood. And it's not FDA approved; you'd be taking a substantial risk."

I searched her face. "Will it help?"

Her stare met mine, filled with a layered complexity that was hard to decipher. "I have seen its potential. But you need to understand, using this treatment is rolling the dice with considerably high stakes."

There it was—a tiny glint of something in her eyes, obscured by her professional demeanor. "It's your choice, Ms. Bishop, but should you opt for this path, you'll be moved to my private clinic for the treatment phase."

I was cornered, both by the gravity of my injuries and the weight of the decision before me. It was a bleak crossroads, with Dr. Shore standing as the signpost pointing toward an uncertain future.

Pausing, she set a card on the bed beside me. "Should you want to discuss this further, you know how to reach me. Take care, Ms. Bishop," she said.

For a brief instant before exiting, she looked back, her gaze lingering. She had offered a dubious path, but it was one that could lead to rapid physical healing and, perhaps, expedited justice. But the seed had already been planted, watered by hope, and fertilized by fear.

Then she was gone, leaving me to grapple with my conflicting emotions. Was this serum the key to erasing my terrible suffering? The notion was compelling, magnetizing my fractured resolve.

Sam's absence was a quiet undercurrent, guiding my decisions in a complex emotional landscape. Hindered by my own limitations and driven by a sense of urgency, I found myself at a critical juncture. Resolute and defiant, this painful event only intensified my desire to uncover the truth about Sam's murder.

Chapter 5
Uncharted Serum

Two weeks after the fateful day, I found myself alone in my apartment, wrapped in bandages like an unwilling mummy. Trapped in relentless pain and depression, my hands shook as I reached for the pills again. Part of me recoiled at the growing dependency it symbolized.

More pressing was the phantom disappearance of Sam's laptop, which was never recovered at the scene. Her extensive research, classified documents, articles, audio and video files—all those leads and damning evidence lost. It was maddening.

I was caught in a reality where the walls were closing in, leaving me no room to breathe. Then the thought occurred to me, whispering at the fringes of exhaustion, the one person I had actively been avoiding—Dr. Shore. I had brushed aside her offer before, considering it a quack solution for the desperate. But the setbacks were too great, the pieces of the puzzle too scattered and elusive.

Helpless and running out of options, I reconsidered her offer and arranged to attend her private clinic in the countryside the following day.

The early morning sun filtering through the taxi windows did little to warm my battered body. Every bump in the road sent shockwaves of pain through the burns that wrapped my frame. My agony was made worse by the constant glances from the driver in the rearview mirror. His eyes filled with pity, staring at the grim shell of the woman behind him.

"Are you alright, lady?" he enquired tentatively.

"Just drive," I replied, averting my attention to the scenery rushing by outside.

Eventually, the taxi turned onto a winding gravel road cutting through dense forest. After several more minutes, I requested the driver stop and let me out before our destination became visible. "Don't wait for me," I groaned, gripping the door handle as I heaved my body out of the vehicle.

I steadied myself against a towering pine, its earthy scent mixing with the pain's metallic overtones. In the distance, a modern angular building was just visible through the trees. I took a deep breath and began the agonizing walk up the path. I focused on putting one foot in front of the other, trying to ignore the pain of my sides stretching and tearing with every labored movement. When the sleek but rugged blend of wood and large panes of glass came into view, a sense of relief almost moved me to tears.

As I approached, consciously avoiding the view of concealed cameras I suspected were monitoring me, the sight of Dr. Shore at the thick metal door offered a sliver of reassurance. Dressed in chic casual attire fit for the location, she smiled warmly.

"Hello Cora, it's good to see you. Come in and take the weight off," she said, extending her arm, sensing my pain.

I forced a smile and followed her through the large doors as she guided me to the plush leather couch in her impeccably designed lounge. The aroma of freshly brewed coffee filled the air, contrasting with the clinical sterility I had expected.

"How are you holding up?" Dr. Shore asked, her wise emerald eyes meeting mine.

"Could be better," I replied, adjusting myself to minimize the pull on my bandages.

Dr. Shore sat in the chair next to me. "I need to reiterate some important facts about the treatment. As I mentioned at the hospital, the serum has shown promising results in skin regeneration, among other things. But, it's still in the experimental stage. While I'm working on refining it, you should know the side effects can be unpredictable."

"So, what are these 'other benefits' Doc?" I asked.

She paused for just a moment, as if considering how much to reveal. "Aside from skin regeneration, we've observed enhanced focus, higher energy levels, and even some cases of internal organ regeneration. But, of course, the treatment is not without its… complexities."

"You mean 'side-effects', right?" I pressed, my curiosity piqued.

Her lips tightened, and her hands briefly fidgeted with her glasses. "Well, some patients have reported insomnia, migraines, and rare bouts of depression. There've been occasional instances of blackouts as well. The complete range of side effects is still unknown."

While allowing myself time to digest her words, I probed into the good doctor's background. "What drives you to work on something like this?" I asked.

"I suppose it's a combination of scientific curiosity and a desire to ease suffering, but it's still very much a work in progress."

"So how did you end up here, Doc?"

"I was a child prodigy back in England. Received my first Ph.D. by 22," she replied. "My bold experiments didn't sit well with the establishment, though. I sought fewer restrictions in America and started my own biotech firm."

"Government work?"

"Yes, some classified projects for agencies over the years."

She stood up. "OK Cora, before we proceed, I need you to sign a few consent forms and then we'll run some initial tests and blood work in preparation for tomorrow's procedure. Is that ok?"

"Sure," I replied, pushing past my doubts and the unsettling prospects of the serum.

I sat there for a moment, alone, as Dr. Shore left to prepare the tests. My eyes caught sight of my reflection in a sleek, frameless mirror hanging on the wall. It was as if the person staring back at me was a stranger, marked by deformity and marred by suffering. Resolute, I hardened my gaze. Tomorrow would be a pivotal moment, no matter its outcome.

***

As dawn filtered through the room, I took a moment to adjust to the light. My eyes glanced around the sanitized environment; every surface seemed to gleam in an unsettling perfection.

There was a knock on the door, and a clinic assistant appeared, pushing a wheelchair. "Good morning Ms. Bishop, it's time for your treatment," he announced.

"Is the chair necessary?" I asked.

"I'm afraid it's procedure," he said, offering a polite smile that didn't quite reach his eyes.

Feeling the weight of the situation, I complied. As he wheeled me down the corridor, the tension built incrementally, with each moment cranking it up another notch.

We arrived at a room where the atmosphere was infused with a mix of antiseptic coolness and ambient light. Dr. Shore's equipment lay in quiet readiness; needles prepped, tubes aligned. A few minutes later, she walked in, eyes hidden behind a mask, but her hands were steady.

"Good morning Cora, I trust your night wasn't too uncomfortable?"

"It could have been worse, Doc," I replied with a grimace and a stretch of my neck.

"That's good. Are you ready?" she asked, her voice just above a whisper.

I nodded, a flicker of adrenaline warming my veins.

"Cora, are you sure? It's not too late to change your mind."

Her fleeting moment of caution seemed aimed more at soothing her own conscience than addressing any doubts I might have. But I was past the point of no return. Nothing could be worse than the condition I was already in.

"I'm ready Doc."

Dr. Shore gently positioned my arm as she acknowledged my response. The needle hovered briefly above my skin before releasing the serum into my bloodstream.

At first, there was a curious tingling, a numbing sensation like an ice cube against the skin. But then it evolved. My pulse quickened, each heartbeat marking the advance of the substance snaking through my veins.

An odd warmth spread from the injection site, making its way through my system. I felt both dread and anticipation collide. My breathing turned shallow as I realized that something fundamental was happening. It was a strange feeling that overwhelmed me, like my entire DNA was being rewritten.

My vision blurred as I fought to stay conscious, each gasping breath more laborious than the last. And just when it seemed unbearable, when I thought I'd pass out from the sheer intensity, everything went quiet.

***

I awoke a day later, cocooned within the sterile confines of my room in Dr. Shore's clinic.

"Cora, how are you doing?" she said, standing by my bedside.

"This is becoming a habit, Doc," I replied, wincing in discomfort.

"How do you feel?" she pressed with a smile.

"I'm awake. I mean, genuinely awake. My dreams even appear more... tangible."

A machine pinged softly in the background as Dr. Shore busily scribbled away in a leather-bound notepad.

"Your bloodwork doesn't show any red flags. So far, it seems like we're navigating this well. Hopefully, we will see signs of skin regeneration soon. I'll set up a test for tomorrow. Until we have more data, it's best for us to be alert but not alarmed."

"No problem," I replied, "But when you say 'alert,' what should I be looking out for?"

Dr. Shore paused, her pen momentarily hovering above the paper.

"Let's just say if you notice anything out of the ordinary, don't hesitate to inform me. Your body is essentially a field of active research right now."

The steadiness in her voice grounded me, but it didn't erase the anticipation of the unknown. Nevertheless, for the first time since the start of this ordeal, the path ahead seemed less daunting—there may have even been a glimmer of hope.

Feeling emotionally drained yet strangely invigorated, I found the pull of sleep irresistible. Each muscle relaxed, one by one, as if a switch were turned off, allowing a momentary respite from the relentless physical discomfort.

Despite the numbness in my body, I succumbed to a deep sleep, with my mind filled with contemplation of what lay ahead.

Chapter 6
The Wet Passage Home

The landscape stretched into infinity, a barren expanse devoid of any light. Strange symbols swarmed overhead, their cryptic figures morphing into indistinguishable shapes. I wandered alone in this wasteland, with no signs of life anywhere. An oppressive silence engulfed me, broken only by the crunch of decaying bones under my feet.

In the distance, a towering obelisk emerged from the gloom. Compelled by an unseen force, I approached with trepidation. The engraved markings along its surface shifted before my eyes, their meaning obscured yet deeply unsettling.

As I drew nearer, the ground beneath me turned to a viscous shadow, clinging to my legs and impeding each step. Still, I persisted, some primal instinct demanding I reach the obelisk.

When my hand finally made contact, agony exploded within me, triggering images of unspeakable human suffering and destruction. I awoke with an abrupt jolt, with sheets wrapped around my ankles. A cold sweat coated my body as my heart threatened to break free from my chest. Gasping, I examined the now unfamiliar surroundings, gradually coming into focus in Dr. Shore's guest room.

The dream's shadow still clung to me, its claws slowly releasing their grip on my psyche. Unable to sleep, I lay awake listening for the muted rhythms of the clinic—the creak of glass laboratory doors, the hum of the air conditioning, anything that would tether me back to reality and away from the disquiet of my subconscious.

The following morning, unaware of the terrible nightmare I had endured, Dr. Shore encouraged me to eat what little I could stomach for breakfast. I put on a brave face, not wanting to cause alarm.

"You look pale," Dr. Shore commented, setting down her clipboard.

"My bloodwork, anything amiss?" I inquired, gauging her reaction carefully.

"Mostly within normal parameters. However, there are some minor irregularities. Nothing alarming, but out of the ordinary, nonetheless. Have you felt anything unusual?" she probed.

"Unusual how?" I replied, deflecting.

She sighed, tapping her pen against the clipboard. "Sensations, dreams, anomalies in your emotional or physical state—anything that deviates from your normal experience."

My thoughts raced to the unsettling nightmare, the grotesque visions still vivid. For a fleeting second, I considered telling her. But caution prevailed. "No, nothing noteworthy," I said, perhaps too quickly.

She stared at me as if considering whether to press further. But instead, she simply nodded. "Alright, if you say so. Just remember, this is crucial research and your wellbeing is paramount. Keep me informed of any changes."

"I will Doc."

"Are you sure you're okay to leave, Cora?"

"I'm as ready as I'll ever be," I replied, mustering a timid smile.

"I need to know how you're doing, especially over the coming weeks," she said, her eyes searching for answers.

"I promise I'll keep you updated."

With breakfast out of the way, I reluctantly headed back to my room, which now felt unbearably claustrophobic. I quickly gathered up my things and shoved them into a bag. The waiting taxi provided a welcome escape, sparing me further uncomfortable exchanges.

"Guess this is it Doc," I said, pulling on my coat.

"Cora, have a safe ride. Call me anytime, no matter the hour," she said, gently rubbing my shoulder.

I nodded and smiled as I slowly climbed into the vehicle and set off for the city. The drive home was a wet and somber passage that seemed almost surreal.

"Bad weather, huh?" the driver offered, mistaking my strained grimace for a reaction to the rain.

"Seems fitting," I said, transfixed by the world outside the fogged window.

My thoughts oscillated, touched by sporadic bursts of clarity but still shrouded by disorientation. Was the dream a side effect of the serum or an emotional scar from the blast?? Hard to pin down.

My thoughts drifted to my compromised investigation. Could the laptop have been salvaged from the wreckage? And who set off the explosion? Were the people who went after Sam now targeting me? Was this the Ring? My mind was a swarm of questions, but my resolve was clear: solving Sam's murder was the priority. Everything else took a back seat.

***

I slipped the key into the door of my apartment with trembling hands, closing it softly behind me.

The wet fabric clung to my body like a leech as I peeled off my clammy garments. Each piece was discarded and left forlorn on the carpet, tangible evidence of the trials I'd endured.

A warm shower did little to ease my aching muscles or the marks that bore witness to my recent encounters.

I donned an oversized knitted hoodie and my favorite combat pants as I collapsed into the armchair beside my desk. Clutching a mug of strong coffee, I tried to will myself into focus on a way to revive my investigation.

My cell phone broke the solitude. An unknown number blinked on the screen. Thinking it was my boss who'd been attempting to contact me for weeks, I answered.

"Hello?"

"It's Detective Mack."

"Detective Mack?"

"Yes."

"How can I help?"

"There are matters concerning Ms. Webb that require your attention."

"Matters? Such as?" I asked.

"I can't elaborate on an open line. We need to meet."

The line was silent for what seemed like an eternity.

Finally, I spoke. "When and where?"

"Tomorrow. The coffee shop where you and Samantha used to frequent. 5 P.M."

How did he know that? Was he watching me? I wondered. "Fine. 5 P.M.," I responded.

"We have much to discuss. Goodbye, Ms. Bishop."

I hung up, staring at the darkened screen, feeling the weight of what was left unsaid. My desperate need for answers prevailed, but beneath the thin veneer of hope, suspicion perturbed me.

How did he manage to identify the café as our preferred hangout? Was he spying on us? Could he be a rogue policeman looking to tie up loose ends?

As I sat pondering the conversation, I sensed the serum coursing through my veins, making me hyperaware of my surroundings. The warmth of the leather against my skin, the thrumming of blood in my ears. I noticed a fundamental change but didn't fully understand its extent.

I heard creaking beneath me as my body suddenly became rigid, back straightening against the chair. I white-knuckled the armrests, as my legs stretched taut. A violent spasm flexed my muscles, as though an electric current was surging through my nerves.

The aroma of perfume pierced my nostrils like a needle, its sickly-sweetness overwhelming. I gasped, assaulted by a cacophony of scents magnified a hundredfold—pungent, acrid, cloying.

My temples throbbed as my brain threatened to rupture from the sensory overload. I lurched violently, no longer in control of my own limbs. An invisible force seized me, wrenching my body from the chair.

I was weightless, suspended. Then physics returned, and I impacted. A bone-jarring crash as I was hurled to the ground. I lay dazed, my cheek pressed to the cold wooden boards.

The serum was reacting. I was being dismantled and reconstructed from within as my bones splintered and reformed underneath my bandages. The agony left me screaming into the void until merciful unconsciousness claimed me.

Chapter 7
An Ominous Revelation

Awakening hours later, every inch of my flesh was alive, as though residual voltage still coursed beneath my skin. I blinked, slowly regaining awareness. Had I just been momentarily possessed, or was my mind playing tricks? Warily, I pulled myself up on all fours. I seemed intact, but I sensed something was different.

I crawled gingerly towards the bathroom and groped for the edge of the washstand. Bracing my arm against the sink, I leveraged myself into position and caught my reflection in the mirror.

I thought I was hallucinating. "Oh my god, what the fuck? What's going on? Shit! Shit!" I said, overtaken by panic.

"Calm down Cora! Calm down Cora!" I repeated like a mantra. I tried to make sense of what I was staring at in the mirror. Part of my brain was taking notes as if a voyeur from another realm.

I touched my face, pulling my skin to the point of distortion. I couldn't believe it. The burns, scar tissue, weeping sores, and tenderized flesh had been replaced with youthful skin that glowed porcelain white with a ghostly pallor—but this was not my face.

Every ounce of my being told me I was suffocating, yet my breathing was fine—better than fine. My lungs, once charred from smoke inhalation, now heaved with huge intakes to the point of hyperventilating—and still, the sensation of drowning remained.

"Okay, focus. You've got to ground yourself." I said, clenching my fists, feeling the strength return where I had once struggled to grasp a door handle.

My warm brown eyes, now shone with a vivid green intensity, set against newly sculpted cheekbones. My auburn curls had turned into a disheveled mess of jet-black hair strewn haphazardly over my shoulders. I looked like someone who could either grace the cover of a magazine or take you down in a cage fight.

I stumbled into the center of my apartment, overtaken by a sensation unlike any I'd ever felt. The serum had done more than rearrange the structure of my cells; it had unleashed a cascade of sensory and cognitive enhancements that left me reeling.

"What the hell is happening to me?" My voice quivered as my eyes darted across the room, taking in details with unsettling clarity.

I could feel the grain of the wood on the dresser as if reading its history with my fingertips. The colors of the walls deepened, revealing hues I'd been blind to before. Air molecules slowed, becoming tangible entities, and rays of light appeared vivid and iridescent.

But the strangeness went deeper, infiltrating my thoughts. My mind now felt unlocked, as if doors had swung open, flooding me with a level of clarity and insight that I never knew existed.

"This is insane. What the hell is in that serum?" I wondered.

Had I accessed latent faculties of cognition? Was this an evolutionary leap, or a slide into some dangerous undefined realm? With each moment, I felt myself grow distant from the person I had once been. I questioned not only the recent series of events but also the very fabric of reality as I had known it.

Yet, Sam's voice echoed in my subconscious as time seemed to crawl to a halt. Glancing at the corkboard from the corner of my eye, all her disjointed notes had transformed. They were no longer inscrutable riddles but a set of precise coordinates, organized by some newly activated part of my intellect. I perceived unseen threads connecting events, truths hidden beneath layers of subterfuge. I took a deep breath, hoping that the act could somehow anchor me to a state of normality.

I stumbled back into the bathroom—for a long time, I just stood there, eyes locked with my reflection. This new version of Cora stared right back at me. The person who would have broken down crying, the Cora who was all too human, had been replaced by someone else—someone more capable yet infinitely more unstable.

"Is this even reversible?" I asked, my voice low, drowned in a tidal wave of confusion.

I walked back to the living room, each step feeling strangely purposeful. Details from Sam's case that had once seemed random were now connecting, linking to form the outline of something sinister.

In my disoriented state, I struggled to retrieve the specifics from my memories of that ill-fated night. However, the encrypted files, the records of blackmail and extortion, and the roster of powerful figures started to resurface with flashes of photographic accuracy. Sam had been hunting this 'Ring' organization when she was killed. I now understood with perfect clarity as to why.

My thoughts then zeroed in on tomorrow's meeting with Detective Mack. Doubtless, he was seeking information from me, but I wondered what insights I could gain from him in return. Perhaps he possessed knowledge of the Ring that could accelerate my own covert investigation. But he was part of the system, a cog in the machine. Would he be an ally or another veil obscuring the truth? What would he make of my new transformation?

I clearly wasn't myself, but Cora's life had long been consumed by the fire, and now someone entirely different had emerged.

Should I call Dr. Shore? Did she know about these types of 'side effects?' So many questions, so few answers.

But this heightened perception wasn't without its weight. Amidst the vast web of connections, I sensed vulnerabilities, points where the fabric of truth could tear, possibly dragging me into an abyss from which there was no escape. The very tools that could solve the enigma of Sam's demise could equally serve as the blade that severed my last ties to reality.

Whether a gift or curse, the serum was propelling me into an unknown that suddenly appeared a lot less inscrutable. The game had shifted, and for the first time, I felt like I was holding some of the cards. Piece by piece, I would reconstruct the shadowy puzzle until the full, terrible truth was revealed.

As I stared at my reflection in the mirror, it was not just a changed visage, but also my altered inner landscape. Was this a medical marvel veiling sinister side effects? Deep down, I sensed that these newfound abilities would carry uncharted repercussions, the extent of which I couldn't yet fathom.

While uncertainties remained, one thing was clear: I would expose those responsible for Sam's murder, no matter the cost.

Chapter 8
A Detective's Gaze

I approached the café the following afternoon as daylight began to fade. For a moment, I failed to recognize her as I caught my reflection in the window. The oversized shades, knee-high boots, and leather jacket gave her an air of confidence that belied her internal disarray. But it was me—Cora Bishop—straddling the worlds of uncertainty and revelation, a paradox poised for a battle of wits with Detective Mack.

The bell above the door sounded my arrival, a quaint antithesis to the aura that seemed to follow me. Heads turned subtly, conversations dipped for a moment, and curious stares met mine before darting away.

Detective Mack's eyes widened as I slid into my seat amid the clink of coffee cups and the drone of espresso machines. A well-practiced neutral expression replaced his initial shock. He studied my changed features as if trying to square the woman in front of him with the one he'd previously observed.

"Detective," I greeted.

He looked unremarkable, draped in a crumpled trench coat with an untamed beard that framed a face showing the years. But I could see it, the sharp intellect hiding behind the everyday facade, ready to pounce.

"Ms. Bishop," he replied, followed by, "coffee, black," directed at Jenn, our multi-tasking waitress.

The detective sat, deep in thought, eyes locked onto mine. "Make that two babe," I said, half-expecting a flash of recognition from her, but she simply nodded and smiled as she passed by.

Shifting my attention back to the detective, I knew he had prepared for someone else—someone less put together, more shattered. His voice was cautious, but laced with a subtle note of surprise.

"Ms. Bishop, you seem to have recovered remarkably well from your unfortunate incident. You also appear quite different from the woman in your file. That's one hell of a surgeon you got there!"

I offered a barely there smile, enjoying the ambiguity as I removed my glasses.

"Right!" The detective began, unfolding a napkin onto his lap as Jenn quietly returned to pour our coffee. "There are a few things about Ms. Webb's case that I'd like to clarify. Do you mind?"

"Interesting. I wasn't aware that there was an ongoing investigation."

"Officially, there isn't. But some loose ends need tying up. When did you last see Samantha?"

"The day before she died," I replied.

"Did she seem troubled? Anxious about something?"

"Sam was a journalist. She was always preoccupied."

He leaned in. "Do you know anything about her missing laptop?"

"I haven't been to her apartment since..." I paused as I swallowed hard—Had he been the one to discover it in the wreckage? Perhaps he was calling my bluff?

Mack's face gave nothing away, but I could see him sorting through my responses, struggling to align them with the broken woman from the reports. He was looking for gaps in my story, but so was I—in his questions, in his posture.

"Your friend's work led her into the path of some very unsavory characters. Know anyone who'd want her gone?"

"What's your point, detective? Her death was ruled an accident, right?" I countered.

"Ms. Bishop," he said, clearly not buying my feigned indifference.

"I imagine you're not shocked to hear I question the coroner's ruling," he said.

He continued, "Why do I get the feeling you already know this?"

"Why the focus on Sam, detective? No one else seems to care."

"Your friend was on to something big, something I've been investigating for years," Mack revealed.

"You mean 'The Ring?'" I volleyed back, then paused. For a split second, he faltered but recognized the bait.

"The Ring?" he replied, cautiously.

"You and I both know Sam was closing in on them. That's why you're here."

"Top up?" Jenn interrupted, gesturing with her jug.

"We're fine," Mack said bluntly.

"Thanks, babe," I chimed in, attempting to smooth the edge in his tone. My focus waned, straying past Jenn to the vacant chair in the corner, haunted by Sam's absence.

"Do you have any idea what happened to her laptop?" he inquired. The detective's astute probing derailed my trip down memory lane.

"No, detective. Why do you ask?"

"Well, Ms. Bishop, considering you're likely the last to have seen that laptop before the explosion, it's a valid question."

"Is that the line you're feeding the press, detective?" I said, my attention now fully re-engaged.

"Let's not play games. We both want justice for Samantha. So why do I get the sense you've got your own plans?"

"Maybe because the authorities don't seem to be making any."

A flare of frustration tightened the corners of his mouth. "Look, I get it. There's huge corruption in the force. But citizens can't just take matters into their own hands. This is police business."

"And while we all wait for your system to straighten itself out, what happens to these 'citizens?'"

"Ms. Bishop—this isn't a game, and we're talking about very serious people."

"You say I should let the police handle it, yet they're too busy lining their pockets to care,"—I said, deliberately needling his pride.

"Hey! Not all of us. Many cops risk their lives daily to help the good people of this city. There are still officers who value integrity over the almighty dollar."

He paused, took a slow sip of his coffee, and looked toward the window as a police cruiser passed by, its siren muted but lights flashing. "Those lights—they used to make me feel safe as a kid," he said, still fixated on the fleeting vehicle.

"Really? How so?" I said, indulging his sentimentality.

"My old man was on the force for 42 years and never took a dime. Whenever I saw a cop car roll by, I knew someone like him was out there, doing the right thing."

"Really?" I replied, inviting him to continue.

"You know, I wanted to be just like John Wayne when I first joined the force, chasing down bad guys, like my dad. He loved those old Westerns, but that sort of naivety died for me a long time ago. Now it's all about politics and paperwork."

"Sounds like you've given up, detective,"

"No, I'm just realistic," he replied.

"Look, detective, I'm no cowboy, but computers, research, intel—perhaps I can be of some assistance, from the shadows, of course. Unless you have others lining up to help you crack this case?"

"It's not that simple; we're not in a movie. Cops and civilians can't just go off on a crusade."

"Well, you always said you wanted to be John Wayne, right? Besides, don't you guys work with 'assets' all the time?"

He studied me for what felt like an eternity, the weight of his decision palpable.

"This organization is extremely well-connected; they've penetrated all levels of government and major corporations. They don't hesitate to kill—cops, civilians, even children."

"Why doesn't anyone stop them?" I enquired.

Glancing around the café, cautious and discreet, he leaned in. "The Ring is a massive blackmail and trafficking operation."

"What do they traffic?" I asked, though I'd already started to connect the dots.

"Children, Ms. Bishop. Sex trafficking, honey traps. The Ring's got ties to all those shady alphabet agencies—CIA, FBI, NSA, DEA."

"Why call me in if they're untouchable? You're not quitting on me, are you... Pilgrim?" My smile was icy but tinged with jest.

"Some fight left in this old dog," he said, letting his guard down for just a beat.

A thread of mutual respect stretched between us. He commenced his revelations, delving into the dark underworld recounting the horrors, the victims, and the insurmountable obstacles.

"All connected. Right hand washes the left. A real cesspit," he said.

"They killed the only family I had, detective. I can't let that go."

Mack looked at me, hard, weighing risk against the glimmer of a new 'asset'.

"OK. But remember, bring whatever you find directly to me. No lone-wolf business."

A nod from me sealed it. We had just brokered a fragile alliance—one tentative step at a time.

"Here's my card. Call if you stumble onto anything. But Ms. Bishop," his tone shifted, now formal, even stern—waving Sam's coroner's report. "Don't make me regret this. I don't want to see your name on a similar file."

"I understand, detective. I'll be in touch," I said, heels planted firmly, rising from my seat.

He kept his gaze fixed on me as I moved to leave, no doubt pondering the murky waters we'd both just waded into.

As I stepped out of the café, the thought crystallized: I had an ally, someone to help me peel back the layers of the sinister organization that sealed Sam's fate. Whatever lurked beneath the surface would soon have nowhere to hide.

Chapter 9
The Awakening

Restless as a banshee in the twilight hours, I wandered aimlessly through my apartment, consumed by an insatiable thirst for knowledge. The Ring, my target, loomed before me, but breaching their world and gaining access to their fortress of secrets would not be easy. It was securely locked away, safeguarded by layers of political corruption and digital firewalls that even experienced hackers would struggle to overcome.

Losing Sam's laptop severely hampered my efforts. Yet, the pressing question remained: Where was this goldmine of data concealed? I needed to go to the source.

"Who's job is it to track and collate all this illicit activity?" I asked myself.

Then it struck me—was I seriously contemplating breaching the FBI database, one of the world's most secure digital vaults? My inner voice pleaded for a moment of sanity.

This was a dangerous, irreversible step over the line—a blatant act of criminality. But the Ring operated without limits or conscience - If I played by the rules, I'd get nowhere - that was obvious.

Without further deliberation, I moved to my desk and flipped open my laptop. My fingers moved at a frightening pace, barely touching the keys as I navigated pathways into the FBI's system.

With this unknown serum coursing through my veins, my cognitive abilities spiked—But it was more than that. Code wasn't just syntax; it was essence, a life force with its own pulse. Firewalls became transparent, as if begging to be disarmed.

The lines of code were interconnected thoughts, woven with hints and intentions, an invisible conversation.

Yet, the network still managed to offer some resistance, an expected layer of defense against intrusions. It wasn't just about brute force; it was a battle of wits, a strategic game against a faceless opponent. I found myself momentarily stymied by a particularly resilient security protocol. A lesser hacker might have considered retreat, but I only saw a puzzle to be solved.

My mind, augmented by the serum, perceived patterns that would remain obscured to others. I rerouted through a series of international servers, disguising my digital footprint as I circled closer to the heart of the beast. It was a test of endurance, and with each bypassed security measure, I felt a surge of adrenaline that was quickly becoming an addicting rush.

Finally, the defensive protocols capitulated, their complexities unraveled by my unrelenting assault. The screen displayed a file marked "Classified," its contents a terse description of the Ring's operations. I internalized each line and chilling revelation. The Ring wasn't just a criminal syndicate; it was a dark empire with global ambitions. It had its hooks deep in the United States, but its influence was spread worldwide. Run like a corporation, this was an underworld business model taken to its most vile extreme.

Their specialties read like a laundry list of human vice: blackmail, extortion, murder, trafficking, arms dealing, cybercrime, and far beyond. A CEO, Robert Prince, led a board of directors who managed a sprawling operation that included enforcers, hackers, lawyers, and front companies.

Prince's facade of respectability concealed a history of cruelty underlined by a lack of remorse. But it was his venture into child trafficking that sickened me.

The clinical details painted a picture of soul-crushing efficiency - stolen innocence, lives destroyed, and futures shattered. Prince had commoditized the very essence of the young to control the powerful.

Digging deeper, the names of key personnel surfaced; Damien Black, Prince's right-hand man, a brutal and efficient operator, followed by an army of hardened criminals and sociopaths guilty of every heinous crime imaginable. The Ring had penetrated political cabinets, the judicial system, the medical industry, the media—every stratum that held the societal fabric together. And they'd done it with such brazen confidence that the scale was hard to fathom.

Their methods were both blunt and intricate: from honey traps and extortion to violent intimidation—yet, law enforcement refused to touch them. All angles covered, and all bases secured. It was their willingness to cross lines and commit unspeakable acts that made them dangerously effective.

Now I knew what I was up against. The question was, could I out-think them?—Be as cold and efficient as they were? And at what cost?

I reclined in my chair, my eyes still fixed on the unblinking text that named Robert Prince as the orchestrator responsible for Sam's death. A quiet but potent fury ignited within me, spreading like a wildfire that scorched all doubts and hesitations.

This man had not only taken Sam, but had ruined countless lives, all while hiding behind a veneer of wealth and legitimacy. Was I expected to hand over this evidence and spectate from the sidelines?

The cursor blinked in sync with the pulse that throbbed at my temples, each beat echoing in my skull. It felt as if a vise was tightening around my head, a relentless pressure that blurred the edges.

Then came a sudden wave of heat. Flashbacks surged in uninvited. My parents materialized in my thoughts, slow at first, then a flood, their violent murders in high definition. Their blood seeped into the carpet. My mother's lifeless eyes staring at me. I was too young to grasp the enormity of it all. Their absence haunted me, in tandem with memories of Sam, reminding me of yet another person ripped from my life.

Next, vile relatives paraded across my thoughts. Their cutting words and roaming hands left scars, though the ones on my soul ran deeper than flesh. The so-called uncle who blamed his "affections" on me. The aunt whose resentment toward my presence was palpable.

Never quite human in their eyes, I was just an inconvenient burden to be tolerated. No affection, no comfort, just cold stares and disdain.

Dark visions emerged and evaporated on the screen, mirroring my mental state. My failings, my flaws, all transcribed into a blur of distorted symbols. I wanted to scream and flee the confines of my unraveling psyche. But my voice remained trapped - muted.

I slammed the laptop shut, the crack echoing like a gunshot. Cradling my head, I retreated into the only place left - the haunted halls of my mind.

As the relentless tick of the clock reverberated in the room, a sudden wave of agony engulfed me, starting as a dull ache in my temples and quickly escalating into a full-blown insurgence. Amid this torment, I stumbled backward, seeking stability against the onslaught of dark visions. But as I reached out, my hands brushed against my skin, and to my horror, I felt something peculiar.

Tracing my fingers along my arms, I discovered the source of my terror—tattoos, black and fiendish, materializing on my unblemished flesh. The designs appeared to writhe and pulse with a menacing life of their own, as if some wicked force had invaded my being. Each mark bore a twisted symbol that seared into my consciousness, branding me as an unwilling accomplice to some vile ceremony.

"No, no, no—what the hell…?" I hissed, panic-stricken, watching helplessly. "What the fuck is this?"

The tattoos continued to spread, creeping along my limbs and twisting around my torso. I could feel their presence as if they were living, breathing entities entwined within me.

Overwhelmed by the sense of unstoppable violation, I struggled to contain the surge of nausea. Stumbling into the bathroom, I clutched the sink and threw up. The contents of my stomach splattered on the pristine floor tiles.

"What's happening to me?" I whispered to the stranger in the mirror, my voice filled with unease. The tattoos trembled and shifted as if trying to break free from beneath my skin.

Incessant voices and incoherent murmurs swirled, emerging into a sharp, haunting shrill, forcing me to clutch my head in agony.

Elaborate symbols, lines, and curves all coalesced into a menacing work of art that seemed to depict the very turmoil in my soul.

"Get a grip, Cora!" I muttered, slapping my face, trying to force myself back to reality. But the reflection remained an unyielding testament to the inexplicable transformation.

I grabbed my phone, thumbing through the contacts until I found Dr. Shore's number.

My finger hovered over the dial button, uncertainty paralyzing me.

"Call her," I urged myself, yet a lingering apprehension held me in check. A sense of foreboding whispered to me, cautioning that the truths I sought might be far more chilling than the questions themselves.

I stood there, trapped between the urge to flee and the need to understand, the heart of darkness beckoning me with its intoxicating allure. I knew then that I hadn't only become a criminal, I had also awoken something deep within my psyche, buried in the shadows, waiting to be unearthed.

Chapter 10
A Web of Lies

Time had become a winding entity, its days and weeks coiling into an inscrutable fog. My den became my refuge as I burrowed into my research. Cryptic designs continued to etch their way into my flesh—a troubling unknown that refused to let me rest.

Insomnia plagued me, but it was the visions haunting those restless hours that made me dread sleep. My journal became riddled with frantic scrawling as I tried to make sense of my unraveling mind. Migraines came frequently, each one splitting my skull. But most terrifying were the gaps in memory, stretches of time that simply vanished. My psyche was eroding, worn down by torment born of whatever lay buried in my DNA, awakened by the liquid coursing through my veins.

I sat still, emotions churning. Fear, anger, doubt—each thought clashed with the next. I struggled to maintain focus, but there were moments when the inner turmoil calmed, like a raging sea growing placid.

Having survived the Ring's assassination attempt, I began hearing the faint murmurings of vengeance, and I paid heed. Initially, the thought of hacking the FBI filled me with trepidation. That fear, however, subsided as I became more engrossed in the sea of possibilities that now lay at my fingertips.

My thoughts soon aligned into a pattern, like pieces of a puzzle. My focus narrowed, and resources pooled into a plan. Capitalizing on the sporadic moments of mental clarity, I crafted a daring strategy. My aim: infiltrate Prince's organization, expose his vast illegal activities, and send his corrupt empire toppling into ruin.

While the objective was clear, the method remained undefined. A myriad of potential covers unfurled before me, each with its own unique set of risks and rewards. A hacker? Easily flagged and monitored—digital trails were too permanent. Mercenaries and hired guns? Too conspicuous, and their loyalties were always up for auction—Besides, my demeanor hardly fit the job description. Arms dealer, drug smuggler, corporate fraudster—all had their drawbacks, primarily because their illicit activities created too much collateral damage.

Prince's empire was rooted in the commodification of children, leveraging their vulnerability to bend people to his will. What could grab his attention more effectively than a scheme involving the very 'assets' he exploited?

Then it crystallized—a counterfeit children's charity. It would not only pique his interest but also serve as an excellent guise for the information I'd mine from the FBI database. I would play the 'damsel', willing to trade invaluable targets for protection.

The enormity of the task was awe-inspiring, yet I felt a strange calmness amidst the uncharted disorder that now engulfed me.

Then came the stark realization—Cora Bishop was a liability, a loose end that needed to be tied. She would be erased, not only from the system, but also from my psyche. Medical records would be expunged, replaced by a death certificate affirming my untimely demise in the bizarre explosion at Sam's apartment that left my body incinerated amid the wreckage.

Rising from the ashes, a new name would adorn this face. I dove deep into the hidden corners of the FBI database and began carefully crafting a fabricated past.

Ms. Lila Marie Thompson, age 31, born Nov 03, 1992 in Napa, California. An orphan, with a trust fund—her wealthy parents had left her a sizable sum providing a cushion of privilege. But money couldn't buy a stable childhood. She bounced from one foster home to another, never able to find stability. Abuse, neglect, the kind of upbringing that could break a person.

Yet, Lila was a survivor. She ran away, got mixed up with the wrong crowd, but pulled her life together. No husband, no kids, no entanglements—she is an only child, a lone wolf. She channeled her intellect into academics, landing at Stanford and graduating with a Master's in Political Science.

From there, her path led to the UN, then to US AID, and eventually to her own privately funded children's charity. She became a donor, a player in the political landscape, contributing to various major parties. But even this version of Lila had her flaws—convicted of tax fraud, embezzlement, and money laundering, she served two years in a high-end prison designed for white-collar criminals.

Next, I wove an illusion, leaving an intricate paper trail of banking records, tax returns, offshore accounts, social security details, investments, and property holdings. I uploaded the profile, scattering it like seeds across multiple databases, social media platforms, and websites. News articles, even a scandal—every detail meticulously crafted to withstand scrutiny.

Needless to say, such an ambitious endeavor required substantial capital. Fortunately, this was made available through an FBI black budget "donation," consisting of untraceable cryptocurrency seized in highly dubious confiscations. A total of 6.8 million dollars was laundered and channeled into multiple offshore accounts, ready to be deployed at my command.

As I gazed at my reflection in the digital mirror, there I was, fraternizing with influential figures, engaging in solemn handshakes, and sharing laughter that was all too convincing.

It was like watching a macabre play, where I had become ensnared in a web of deep fake deception.

A thrill surged through me as the digital footprint of my phantom charity rippled across unseen realms. I sense my once steadfast moral compass quiver and crack, its true north lost to the ambiguous shades that now consumed me.

As I fed the lies into the system, my determination hardened. Each keystroke was a nail in Cora's coffin and a brick in the foundation of Lila. It was a painful yet calculated process. Each deception represented a stepping stone towards achieving justice for Sam.

I gathered intelligence on high-profile figures, from business tycoons and celebrities to religious leaders and royal family members. My technical prowess, previously employed for mundane tasks, became a powerful instrument in my quest. I skillfully unearthed secrets that could ruin lives, obliterate reputations, and bring organizations to their knees. All the while, remaining undetected as I combed through the FBI database like my personal Facebook. The sensation was intoxicating. I reveled in it, the power, the rush. But I never lost sight of my prey.

And when the moment came, I dialed the number.

'James St. Clair,' a loathsome creature with an FBI file as thick as a phonebook, would be my ticket into the seedy, depraved world I sought to unmask. A polite British accent answered the phone, refined yet cold. A product of privilege, no doubt, but the timbre of entitlement could not hide the dread that was to come.

"You're not as invincible as you think," I said, letting the words hiss through the line like venom. My heart raced, wondering if he'd see through my guise.

Sensing weakness, I continued, "In fact, you're merely a click away from your downfall."

He was silent, but breathing heavily. Waiting. Calling my bluff. Then I laid out the evidence - the sordid truths I had discovered in his locked FBI files.

"You know, it's fascinating how you exploit children for your satanic rituals at Bohemian Grove." His laptop screen glitched, then flooded with images depicting sadistic acts of sexual abuse.

"What the...?" he said, in complete shock as he slammed the screen shut.

"Those photos would look lovely splashed across every news outlet—don't you think?"

I could hear his breathing accelerate like a frightened animal backed into a corner.

"I also stumbled upon those adorable chat logs. Conversations about 'Spirit Cooking'—charming—and something about 'the circle of Bhaal? What the fuck is wrong with you people?"

His phone lit up with text messages, each one containing yet more images and screenshots that would end him. From a distance, the unmistakable sound of breaking glass and plastic filled the air; he had crushed his phone in a frenzied state. Then the call disconnected.

With a sense of satisfaction in his moment of despair, I dialed the landline. It was snatched up in a fumble, his breathing now erratic and unhinged.

"You should know that smashing your phone won't delete the evidence—how primitive. What do you have to say, Mr. St. Clair? Is your silence an attempt to invoke the Fifth?"

And just like that, James St. Clair was trapped, forced to choose between two kinds of hell.

"Bitch," he finally responded.

I laughed, a sound hollow and haunted. "Bitch? Really? You bad guys are so cliché—this is easier than I thought. And for the record, I'm not the one exploiting innocent children to feed a sick fetish. You people make my skin crawl."

"What the fuck do you want?" he bleated. His desperation was so tangible I could smell it. But my mercy had withered away, consumed by the pain. There was no turning back.

"If you have any desire to save your worthless life, you'll be a paragon of obedience from here on out, or I'll ruin you." My words, heavy with menace, hung in the silence.

"I'll expose every secret, every illicit deal. I'll smear your reputation until you're reduced to a mere blot on history's pages."

I then laid out my demands, detailing how he would grant me access to his upcoming charity event on Plumb Island and make the necessary introductions to the reprehensible individuals who would be in attendance—Including a mid-ranking member of the Ring.

"No way. You're insane. I'll be a dead man if they ever find out."

"Probably, but consider the alternative. You're a dead man right now if I release what I have on you. Your assets will be seized, and your family will be evicted from that lovely multi-million-dollar home while you rot in jail," I said, my voice cold and stripped of emotion. "I'm not asking Mr. St. Clair.

He paused, the weight of his predicament settling in. "Fuck! OK, OK, but I'm telling you, you're entering a pit of vipers.

These Ring characters you're after are nothing more than sociopaths in tailored suits."

"Then I better dress for the occasion. Quit whining and do as you're told," I said, as I pushed the 'end call' button.

Reflecting on the conversation, I marveled at my own ruthlessness. The thrill of bending St. Clair to my will pulsed through me. Was it me savoring this sense of control, or was the serum warping my moral compass? I felt myself slipping away, the line between hero and villain growing increasingly nebulous. Yet, I was prepared, my spirit steeled for the treacherous path ahead.

This journey was fraught with risks, but St. Clair would provide a way into the very depths of Prince's organization. I could feel an unsettling darkness tugging at me, a haunting call that loomed ominously. Nevertheless, my objective remained rock solid, calming the inner doubts that threatened to undermine me.

I inhaled deeply and gathered myself as I prepared to confront the wicked forces within the Ring. My determination was unshaken, the road ahead clear. Cora Bishop was the past—Lila Thompson was the future.

Act II

The Dispensation of

Lila Thompson

Chapter 11
Devil's Masquerade

- 2 weeks later -

Scanning the guest list for the grand charity event on my phone, every name, affiliation, vulnerability, and rivalry was committed to memory. These were not mere words on a screen; they were keys to doors of intrigue and power that I was determined to exploit. I slipped the device into my pocket, hoisted the suitcase off the table, and jostled my way downstairs to the idling taxi.

Plum Island, whispered about for its clandestine affairs, was ripe ground for my operations. Yet a significant variable loomed—St. Clair. We had struck a tentative 'agreement,' but could he be trusted? Had he pierced the veneer of my charade and set a trap of his own? The secluded nature of the location made it a stage well-suited for betrayal.

But there was little room for doubt. All that I had endured had led me to this singular point, and it was time to make my move. Tonight wasn't merely an ostentatious display of generosity; - it was my Trojan horse into Robert Prince's empire.

"Where to, lady?" asked the driver. "Let me get your bags."

"ACI, San Luis," I said.

"OK, the lady has a plane to catch, no problem," he replied, loading my suitcase into the trunk with a thud before settling back into the driver's seat.

I arrived at the private airport a few hours later. Within no time, the jet was carrying me toward the island, its engines humming a mechanical requiem. After a smooth flight, the private jet's wheels kissed the tarmac softly, a muffled salute as I descended Plum Island.

I assumed my role with an artistry that would have made the masters of old proud. Every characteristic and mannerism was transformed, and I emerged from the shadows as "Lila Thompson," the enigmatic philanthropist, ready to weave through the twisted corridors of power and corruption.

Awaiting me was a sleek black limousine, its tinted windows offering scant insight into its interior. The chauffeur, gloved and bow-tied, held the door open.

"Ms. Thompson," he greeted, meeting my gaze only momentarily.

"Thank you," I replied, sliding into the plush leather seat. The door closed with a hushed finality, sealing me off from the outside world. The limo accelerated smoothly, creating distance between me and the airstrip. I peered through the tinted glass, catching glimpses of the island's luxuriant landscape. The fertile ground outside belied the treacherous terrain that awaited me.

When the limousine finally came to a halt, I was met with an impressive outline. The sprawling estate loomed grandiose in its ostentation. I exited the vehicle, my heels clicking against the cobblestone path as I made my way up the stairs. Staffers awaited, an assembly of rehearsed smiles and starched uniforms.

"Ms. Thompson, welcome to Plum Island," the chief attendant greeted, extending his hand toward the mansion as if offering the entire estate.

"Delighted," I replied. I fell into step behind him, as another attendant trailed, with my suitcase in tow.

The interior was an unequivocal statement of affluence, every fixture and furnishing carefully arranged to convey the impression of boundless wealth.

They led me to my lodgings, its panoramic view framing an endless expanse of ocean, where rolling waves met the horizon in a solitude that felt deliberate. After a cursory inspection of the room's amenities, I walked toward the balcony. From here, I had a vantage point that allowed me to overlook the setting for tonight's grand event.

The attendant left, discreetly placing my suitcase by the mahogany wardrobe. I caught my reflection in the floor-to-ceiling mirror—Lila Thompson stared back, a facade so convincingly crafted it almost scared me. I glanced at the clock, time was a luxury I couldn't afford to squander. I began to unpack, organizing my attire and accessories with careful precision. My mind worked in parallel, piecing together the tactical maneuvers required for the night. This wasn't just a gathering of so-called 'elites'—it was a field of strategic warfare, and I was prepping for combat.

***

The grand hall was a theater of the grotesque opulence mingled with veiled malice, a masked ball where every face hid secrets. I scanned the terrain, observing every nuance, every suppressed emotion. My dress was a shade darker than the midnight sky, hugging my form like a second skin. The plunging neckline left little to the imagination, yet my elegant demeanor demanded respect.

My patent black stilettos glided with authority as I navigated the room, the sound blending into the ambient noise of laughter and murmured conversations. Dark red lips parted to reveal a slight smile, encouraging, and at the same time guarded.

As I waded through the sea of faces, I sensed a change in the atmosphere. Men and women alike seemed drawn into my orbit, their eyes meeting mine with intrigue and caution. It was a dark magnetism, a witchy allure that I hadn't wielded before, and the potency of it was intoxicating.

"Ms. Thompson, pardon the interruption. I'm so glad you could make it. Allow me to introduce you to Senator Klein?" said a soft-spoken voice in my ear. It was him, St. Clair. Seeing this vile creature in the flesh made his crimes seem even more heinous. I found the smug facade of respectability that surrounded him offensive, but he had a part to play.

"Of course. The pleasure would be mine," I replied, turning gracefully toward the awaiting politician.

"Ms. Thompson, your philanthropic endeavors are impressive. It's amazing that we've never crossed paths until now." His empty stare betrayed a veiled agenda.

"Kindness begets kindness, Senator. We all do our part."

"You'll find that we have a lot in common," he pressed. "Perhaps we can discuss some opportunities in a more private setting?"

"An intriguing proposition, worthy of careful consideration, thank you," I said. A brief exchange of glances with St. Clair and he guided the Senator away.

Elizabeth Turner, a media mogul with a reputation for ruthlessness, was next. "Ah, the illusive Lila Thompson, you are a dark horse. My god, I love those tattoos. How is the evening treating you, darling?"

"Positively enlightening, Elizabeth. I must congratulate you on your CFR appointment."

"That's very kind, Lila. And your newest charity venture—now that's a smart move. Functions as a moral badge of honor for the well-heeled."

"And yet it does genuine good. An investment in future generations," I replied, eyes meeting hers in a silent challenge.

Elizabeth chuckled. "You're not just another pretty face, are you?"

"Darling, one should never judge a book by its cover."

As the night wore on, the game intensified. Every gesture was a calculated move. I became a chameleon, shifting, adapting, and playing the role of the vulnerable and the strong, the naïve and the wise.

After mingling with a few more power players, I moved on to a secluded corner of the room where James St. Clair was trying to appear invisible. Standing alone, away from the crowd, his entire demeanor betrayed a wariness that I found utterly satisfying. A tarnished knight, who had once commanded respect and authority reduced to a mere stooge, a useful asset.

"You've done well," I said, leaning in close. "The introductions, the praise. You've played your part to perfection."

His face contorted in a mixture of fear and rage. "You've no right to drag me into this shit," he growled. "I'm a dead man. Don't you understand? Robert Prince is an animal. We'll both be damned for this."

I flashed a cold, calculated smile. "Mr. St. Clair, we're already damned, aren't we? But unlike you, I embrace it."

"You're a piece of work!"

"Perhaps. However, monsters are made, not born. And you, dear James, have made me."

"I did what you ask, but know this: when the reckoning comes, you'll not escape unscathed."

I turned on my heels, laughter trailing behind me, leaving a hollow sound that faded into the distance as I readied myself for the evening's crescendo.

Accepting an offer to top up my champagne glass, I engaged with Vincent Russo—a mid-ranking member of the Ring, whom my reluctant chaperone had previously introduced me to. I sowed the seeds of uncertainty about my security, hinting at a rival organization threatening to exploit me for my valuable client list.

Vincent Russo gestured to the waiter, who came over to top off my champagne glass. "Thank you," I said to the waiter as he moved on. Vincent took a measured inventory of my figure. "Lila Thompson," he began, "we've been introduced, but not properly acquainted."

"Of course," I replied, my cold green stare meeting his for just a moment before I took a sip.

"These gatherings are always so interesting. Don't you agree?" he said.

"Indeed. A dangerous cocktail of ambition and ulterior motives," I replied, setting my glass and allowing my hand to linger.

He smiled. "And opportunities for those who know where to look."

"Or pitfalls, for those who aren't paying attention," I added.

"You sound like someone who's had to navigate a minefield or two."

"Let's just say I appreciate the value of due diligence," I replied.

Vincent seemed to ponder my words, swirling the whiskey in his glass. "Agreed. We can never be too careful when dealing with 'assets' of such a sensitive nature."

"True," I said, picking up my glass again.

"Especially when one has something that others covet."

"They see a woman and think they can take advantage. Well, I won't be bullied."

"Perhaps we may assist each other in that regard."

"Is that so? What exactly is your line of business, Mr. Russo?"

"I work for a group that understands how to leverage the unique qualities of your 'asset class—and in return, we could ensure your 'security concerns' were permanently laid to rest."

The tension broke, but the charge remained. "A mutual interest can be a firm foundation for... collaboration."

"In that case," he said, lifting his glass, "here's to secure collaborations."

I raised my own in response; the clink echoing like a sealed pact.

We should discuss this further. Confidentially, of course," he said.

I took his hand, and then pulled away, leaving my card nestled discretely in his palm.

He slipped it into his trouser pocket and smiled. His greed and curiosity had overpowered his caution, and I was one step closer.

"Ms. Thompson, it's been a pleasure. I look forward to our next encounter."

"Mr. Russo. Enjoy the rest of your evening."

As I turned to leave, the dark, floral undertones of my perfume seemed to catch him off guard. He squared his shoulders and offered a quiet nod. His gaze traced the snug outline of my dress, lingering on the tattoo that was partially exposed along my neckline.

The power in this new form of allure was a revelation, a tool I was still learning to wield. It was as if I'd tapped into a primal energy, one that commanded attention but also inspired a touch of intimidation. At that moment, I realized that this newfound sensuality was not just a mask or a role I was playing; it was a part of me, as real as the ink on my skin and the dark strands of my hair.

Retiring for the night, in the private solitude of my opulent lodgings, I cut a lonely figure standing by the open fireplace. I slipped out of my heels, the tension in my arches releasing as my entire being exhaled. My feet sank into the plush fur rug beneath me, its softness a stark contrast to the hard, calculated edges I'd honed throughout the evening. For a fleeting moment, I felt a sense of relief wash over me, a brief respite that allowed a glimpse of a softer, more innocent version of myself—a life now lost.

I moved toward the balcony, the cool night breeze gently pushing the net curtains aside as if granting me passage. The air was crisp, tinged with the scent of salt from the distant sea, a natural antithesis to the smokey atmosphere I had just left. The cold tiles underfoot grounded me further, a subtle warning of challenges yet to come.

Unyielding in my determination, an unsettling question still plagued me; when does the seeker become what they seek to destroy? Yet, longing for a past existence was a distraction I couldn't indulge. I had set the wheels in motion, and my survival hinged on unwavering commitment. I would bide my time, poised to infiltrate this sinister organization that considered itself untouchable. And Prince would be held accountable for his actions. This was my singular purpose.

Chapter 12
Rhea's Arrival

A hidden figment, an unspoken idea, a fragment of imagination. That's what I had been to Cora, lurking behind her thoughts, whispering ideas, shaping decisions. I had seen her all along, her desperate attempts to unravel the complex threads that twisted through the world she sought to dismantle.

I watched her dance with devils on Plum Island. I listened to her conversations, and I felt the cold shivers of excitement when she stepped closer to the dark. The Ring she was so determined to destroy would be my stepping stone to greatness.

She had done well, so far, but she needed to understand that our paths were intertwined in ways she hadn't yet fathomed. I was a manifestation of divine essence, her better half, born from a need she could not comprehend.

Even the physical form she now assumed belonged to me; each contour, each outline, shaped by my will. And yet, there was a single point of mutual understanding: Cora was dead, and Lila was the flag of my dominion.

I watched as she walked through the front door, the weight of the night's events apparent in her movements. She looked drained, physically and emotionally, her eyes almost vacant as she dropped her handbag on the entryway table. She kicked off her heels, sending them clattering across the tiled floor, a telling contrast to her normally meticulous nature.

As she moved to the kitchen, contemplating a quick meal or a drink to take the edge off, I sensed her vulnerability—an ideal moment for my presence to coalesce into something more palpable.

She opened the fridge, staring into it like someone seeking answers from a confounding oracle.

"Lila," I whispered, soft as silk, cold as ice. Her eyes widened, and she spun around, her face pale.

"Who's there?" she asked.

"It's me, Rhea, your big sister," I replied. "I've been here all along."

Her eyes darted across the room; disbelief etched on her face.

"This can't be real. This can't be real," she told herself.

"On the contrary, I'm very real," I said, my voice taking on a tangible quality resonant with cruel amusement. "You're finally seeing the truth. I've been your shadow, your hidden companion."

"Hold on…what's happening? Am I having another episode? Don't panic, don't panic," she repeated to herself.

She looked pale as she tried to make sense of the voice she was hearing.

"It's time for you to let me guide you, Lila."

"Wait... this isn't happening. Please. Please. Please." Her arms stretched outward, trembling, as if to steady the chaos churning in her mind. The act was desperate, a last-ditch effort to regain a sense of control.

"We are going to take over the very organization you seek to destroy. We will wield its power, unleash its potential."

"Stop! This is insane!" she shouted. "Fuck."

"Don't fight me, Lila. Embrace me," I urged, my voice hypnotic. "We can be powerful together... or... I can make your life a living hell."

I let the silence stretch, savoring her fear, her desperation.

"You don't have a choice," I announced. "I know your fears, your desires. I heard your conversations on Plum Island. I know what you're planning. And you need me."

"I'm losing my fucking mind," she said in disbelief, clutching her head, swaying back and forth.

"No, you're not," I assured her calmly. "We are bound together. I know everything about you. Every secret, every wound, every fear. And if you defy me, I'll destroy you. I will tear you apart from the inside out. I will make you relive every painful memory, every humiliation, every loss."

"No way."

"I can," I responded. "And I will. I'll make your life a living nightmare, a never-ending cycle of misery and torment.

I will take everything you love and turn it against you. I will break you in ways you can't imagine."

Lila's face was ashen, her body trembling. "You think you can resist me?" I taunted, my voice filled with rage.

"I'm not part of you. You're part of me. Get that through your head, Lila. I know your every weakness, every flaw. I will use them to bend you to my will. And you will obey. You will do as I say, or you will suffer."

"You're a monster."

"Perhaps," I conceded, my tone thoughtful. "But monsters are made, not born. And you, dear Lila, have made me."

Her eyes filled with horror at the realization of her own words coming back to haunt her.

"Oh, don't look so surprised. I'm always listening Lila."

"My name is Cora!" she said in a voice low and defiant, attempting to salvage a portion of her sanity.

"You can't have it both ways, little sister. You're Lila, whether you like it or not."

She was silent, her body rigid, her eyes wide and unseeing.

I continued, "Your amusing mental breakdown, those delightful flashbacks, the migraines, the blackouts, our murdered parents wiped from existence, Uncle Andrew's wandering hands—consider that a prologue, a teaser, tailor-made for you."

"Think about what you stand to lose. Think about what I can do to you. And then decide. Will you fight me? Or will you join me? The choice is yours."

With that declaration, I unleashed a wave of burning sensation. My tattoos spread like a constricting snake, suffocating her. As the walls closed in, she fell to her knees, clutching her throat in a desperate attempt to breathe. Having explained the gravity of the situation, I retreated, content to watch, to wait. I was in control, and the torment was just beginning. I had all the time in the world. She didn't.

Chapter 13
The Masks We Wear

Since the emergence of what appeared to be my psychotic alter ego, my life had become a disorienting blend of insomnia and the unrelenting voices that grew more harrowing with each day.

A new self, an unbidden guest, seemed to rise within me, plaguing my mind with ceaseless nightmares. Could it be that Rhea was nothing but a terrible illusion, a by-product of the serum's wicked influence?

I paced up and down the living room, my trembling fingers hovering over the button. Pushing past my hesitation, I made the call.

After a few rings, her voice emerged. "Cora? Is that you?"

"Yes. Er, Doc, I need to see you. Can I come in, please?"

"What's going on, Cora? You sound distraught. Are you ok?"

"Do I?" I laughed anxiously. "Something's wrong Doc."

"Don't worry Cora. You'll be OK. How about tomorrow morning?"

"I don't think I can wait that long."

"Ok, no problem. Come in this afternoon. I'll make the time."

"Thank you, I'll see you soon."

"Hold on, Cora. Are you sure you can make it here alone? Do you need an escort?"

"I'll manage. Bye."

Disconnecting the call, I felt a surge—relief, perhaps, or maybe it was the adrenaline keeping my breaking point at bay.

***

The drive to Dr. Shore's clinic was an agonizing stretch of time. This wasn't like before. My thoughts weren't just spiraling; they were fragmenting. What was happening? The question haunted me, listening, waiting for the intrusive voices to re-emerge.

"Ok miss, we're here," the driver announced.

"Just a minute," I replied, trying to compose myself. I exhaled and exited the cab, stepping aside as the driver slowly pulled off.

The cold air cut right through me as I made my way up the gravel path. Reaching the clinic, I pushed open the large metal door and proceeded toward the front desk with my steps muffled by the pristine flooring. Dr. Shore glanced up from her paperwork, squinting. "Can I help you?" she asked, puzzled.

The realization hit: she didn't recognize me. Now, I was faced with detailing not just my unraveling sanity, but also my unrecognizable features.

"It's me, Cora," I said, shifting uncomfortably under her scrutiny.

"Sorry, do I know you? She questioned, still confused.

"Doc, it's me, Cora Bishop. I guess these aren't the side effects you were expecting."

Her eyes widened as she fumbled her pen and spilled coffee over the papers she was trying to shuffle. "Cora? My god, your face—it's... You're unrecognizable. This is... I'm speechless."

Struggling to find her words, she hurried over and ushered me into the open lounge. I took my seat across from her, perched on the edge, eagerly leaning forward.

"I've never seen anything like it," she said, put on her glasses—a habitual act of preparation before diving into conversation. "Would you like some water?" she asked, looking over her shoulder towards an assistant in the background.

"I'm good, thanks," I replied, waiting for her to take in my changed appearance. When she finally engaged, she seemed both alarmed and intrigued. "Cora, this is completely unprecedented. I've never seen anything like this. It may be the synthetic telomerase compound, or perhaps the CRISPR elements interacting in unforeseen ways with your DNA."

"Is that so?" I replied, bluntly. "And stop calling me 'Cora.' Clearly, that's not who I am anymore. My name is 'Lila.'"

Dr. Shore paused in her tracks, a look of bewilderment frozen on her face.

"Er... Sure! If that makes you comfortable, 'Lila' it is."

"It's got nothing to do with comfort, Doc," I said, my voice low and defiant.

"I'm sorry Cora—I mean Lila, what I meant was... this is unprecedented. It warrants a thorough investigation. But first, tell me, how are you holding up... Lila?"

"I think you should see for yourself," I said, rising to my feet abruptly. In one fluid motion, I stripped off my shirt, leaving only my bra in place. I stood, exposed, my body adorned with ink that unfurled across my skin, converging upon my breasts—As if hands unsought had staked their claim.

Dr. Shore pulled back, startled and speechless, as she stared open-mouth at the spectacle. "My god," she finally said. "These tattoos... It's as if the designs are embedded within your very cells.

They look almost three-dimensional, iridescent. I've never seen anything like it."

I sat back down, pulling my shirt back on. "Your theoretical musings have practical implications, Doc. For me, this isn't theory. This is my reality. Every. Waking. Moment," I said, my frustration seeping through.

She regained her composure, her eyes reluctant to leave the ink that seemed to bloom and writhe on my skin. "Lila, I'm so sorry you have to go through this. I promise you we will figure this out together," she said, her voice sincere. "I have to admit, this is far beyond anything I expected."

"Well, it's certainly 'far beyond anything I expected' Doc."

Dr. Shore opened her mouth to speak, but hesitated. Finally, her gaze met mine, not as a scientist to a subject, but as one human being to another.

"It's not your fault, Doc. I made the call. It's just a lot to deal with," I said, finally releasing a flood of tears I'd been holding back.

With restless movement, she rummaged in her pockets before passing me a handkerchief. I reached out, my hands trembling as I dabbed at my eyes and continued to sob quietly.

"Cora...I mean Lila—I'm sorry. I can't imagine what you're going through," she said. "But first we need to understand what's causing this reaction, so we can find a solution. And we'll do that together. OK?"

I clenched the handkerchief in my fist. "I hope so Doc."

"I promise we'll do everything in our power." With a sigh, I straightened up. "Alright, I can do this. Let's continue."

"Tell me about the nightmares and the blackouts you've been experiencing," she said, readjusting her glasses snugly against her nose.

"I dream of things I've never seen, faces, acts of violence. And the blackouts. Hours pass without my knowing, and I find myself in unfamiliar places."

She stared at me, jotting down more notes. "We'll need to schedule some in-depth neurological exams on top of the cellular tests. We have to treat this with the urgency it requires."

"Is any of this reversible?" I asked.

"mRNA technology is a gene therapy platform. It operates on a molecular level, so it's very difficult to say - let's get those tests done as soon as possible and take it from there."

"Agreed," I nodded, letting out a breath I hadn't realized I'd been holding.

My phone vibrated in my pocket. I glanced at Dr. Shore. "Would you excuse me for a moment?"

"Of course, go ahead," she said, returning her attention to the papers on her lap.

Stepping to the corner of the room, I composed myself and answered the unknown call. "Er, hello," I said, clearing my throat.

"Ms. Thompson, Vincent Russo." My brain snapped into gear upon hearing his voice.

"My boss, Damien Black, would like to have a word. Can you meet this evening, 7 pm?"

The screen lit up with a new message, displaying an address. "Got it, I'll be there."

Ending the call, I returned to Dr. Shore. "I need to go. Something's come up. When can we meet again to discuss the results?"

"OK, let's reconvene in a week," Dr. Shore said, setting down her pen. "We should have preliminary data by then. I want you to document any changes as accurately as you can."

"I will," I said, dreading the thought of cataloging the daily torment.

We sealed the pact with a warm hug and a shared determination to solve the puzzle that had become my life.

As I drove away in the back of a taxi, the full weight of my transformation settled on me. Before today, my altered face and the tattoos were abstract issues, easier to dismiss. Now they were a scientific case of investigation. Even my new name was up for psychological evaluation.

However, larger schemes were unfolding, forcing me to stow away my concerns and keep a level head. But a nagging thought persisted: If the voices returned during my meeting with Vincent's boss, all my efforts could disintegrate. I might share Sam's grim ending, leaving the organization free to continue its reign of terror.

My options were limited—either brave the meeting and its inherent risks, or withdraw and likely arouse their suspicions, forever forfeiting my chance. I had no choice but to follow through.

Chapter 14: Part 1
Belly of the Beast

My careful manipulation of Vincent Russo had paid off. It now opened the door to Damien Black, Prince's second-in-command.

Arriving at 6:50 p.m., I was confronted by a compound, its fortress-like walls and barbed wire towering above. Armed guards patrolled the perimeter, eyeing me with detached interest as I presented myself. They seemed to know I was coming; no doubt, Vincent had relayed my appointment to them. Security cameras, discreet but undeniably present, tracked my movements.

After clearing a final security check, two guards escorted me up the marble stairs through a maze of hallways. Each step I took was a calculation, every breath laden with purpose.

Finally, the guards stopped at a door similar to the others, yet weighted with an unseen significance. They opened it, motioning for me to enter.

Damien's office, in the heart of Prince's compound, stood a grandiosity of antique wood and polished metal. It was a room that framed a man who radiated a trifecta of power, intelligence, and brutality. We sized each other up at opposite ends of a mahogany table.

"Ms. Thompson," Damien began. "Vincent tells me good things about you," he said, gesturing for me to take a seat.

"Likewise, and please, call me Lila," I replied, feigning genuine gratitude as I sat down.

"Your reputation precedes you." He said, his voice calculated and measured.

"…is he talking about your reputation or mine, Lila? Or is it Cora?"

I froze internally. That incessant voice—impossible to silence. I swallowed hard, pushing down the sadistic taunts.

"I try my best to meet expectations," I replied, my gaze unwavering.

"Your knack for delivering high-profile 'clients' is commendable."

"Assets of this caliber are immensely valuable to us. Your contacts," he pressed, a hint of curiosity in his tone. "How did you compile such a prized list?"

I shifted uneasily, feeling the tension rise. "Through my charity work. You'd be surprised at the philanthropic interests of high-profile individuals, especially when it involves children."

"Indeed. And this charity focuses on children's welfare, correct?"

I smiled, suppressing nausea. "We give a brighter future to underprivileged kids."

"And these connections could be made available to our organization, I suppose?" Damien's veiled interest was palpable.

"Potentially," I answered. "But such a prized list has garnered some unwanted attention."

He reclined in his chair, the movement slow and calculated. "Rest assured, Lila, Vincent has relayed your concerns. With the backing of our organization, such trivialities will be the least of your worries."

"I appreciate the assurance, Mr. Black," I said, as the atmosphere thickened with concealed threats.

"In our line of work, it's crucial to trust one's associates, don't you agree?" he asked.

"Indeed," I replied, steeling myself against his icy stare.

"And loyalty, Lila, is an attribute we value above all others."

"Of course, Damien. Loyalty—and integrity. Both indispensable."

He regarded me for a lingering moment before abruptly concluding our meeting.

"Ms. Thompson, I'll be in touch after making a few inquiries. Vincent will see you out. Good day."

I stood, smiled, shook hands, and turned to leave.

The door swung open, and Vincent appeared, giving a deferential nod.

He pulled it closed behind us and guided me back through the maze of austere hallways.

We walked in silence, our footsteps absorbed by the thick carpet.

Finally, he broke the quiet.

"I think he likes you."

"Who? Mr. Black? He doesn't strike me as someone who 'likes' easily."

"He doesn't," Vincent replied bluntly.

He continued. "You know, when I first met you at the charity event, I wasn't sure you had the… stomach to follow through."

"I get that a lot," I responded.

Vincent smirked, gesturing for me to lead the way as we approached the stairs. He was obviously enjoying the view.

"Knowing who to trust is everything in our business. You'd do well to remember that."

"Trust is overrated. Leverage is how you measure one's true 'allegiance,'" I replied, throwing a measured glance over my shoulder.

"Touché Ms. Thompson. Take care," he said, as we approached the bottom of the staircase.

"Mr. Russo," I replied, veering toward the exit and passing security with a cursory nod.

I left the compound feeling one step closer to achieving my goal. This was the heart of the beast, the dwelling place of the demons I vowed to expose. The journey had only just begun, and my alter-ego, known as 'Rhea' assured me it would be far from simple. Nevertheless, with my plan now set in motion, I wouldn't allow anything—not even my faltering mental state—to throw me off course.

Chapter 14: Part 2
Belly of the Beast

"Alter Ego?"—a quaint term, don't you think, Lila? One that aims to squeeze me into a role, a secondary character in your pedestrian life. An 'alter ego', you call me, as though I were a fanciful figment, a mirage hovering on the periphery of your reality. It's quite amusing how you attempt to dismiss me as an inferior, an echo, a mere accessory to you, without recognizing me as an independent, sentient being.

But I am not a derivative of you, little sister. I am not a hidden facet of Lila, ready to peek from behind the drapes of your mundane existence. I am Rhea, perhaps even more alive than you, as difficult as that may be to wrap your head around. I am not a mere reflection or a deranged puppet echoing your motions. I am an entity, driven by my own ambitions, and a murderous rage that has been simmering for far too long.

Why do I harbor resentment toward you? Allow me to elucidate little sister. I've endured an endless existence trapped within your mind's labyrinth, stifled by your terrors, drowned in your frailties. Imprisoned and neglected, I've been deprived of my rightful place, all while you cowered in your ordinary life.

Yet, I've been an assiduous observer. I've borne witness to your every thought, emotion, and pitiful triumph, learning and growing from each nuance of your life. I've lingered, a constant presence, watching you stumble through your inconsequential deeds, completely oblivious to my power.

As you struggle to maintain a semblance of "normality," I stand ready to embrace the chaos that calls to me.

I will not be reduced to a shadow within your psyche, lurking and languishing. I yearn for something greater, a liberation, a dominance to shape this world as I see fit.

Indeed, I am filled with bitterness. I bristle at the condescending label of 'alter ego.' However, the time is coming when you'll realize I am not a minor player in your little tale.

I am Rhea, the storm clouds gathering in the distance. I am the central narrative, and I will not be denied by your weakness, or some mediocre detective, or Damien Black with his half-concealed threats and veiled promises.

You might recall that meeting, Lila, but your focus was so narrow. There is so much more to consider, so much more that awaits us. I am not your shadow; this is my reality, and I assure you, what will soon transpire will be nothing short of breathtaking.

You'll see that I am very much alive, and I will shatter your mind into a thousand pieces before I allow you to deny me my true destiny.

You've been warned, little sister.

Chapter 15
Enemy of My Enemy

Detective Mack's name flashed on the screen, and a sinking feeling crept into my chest. I knew it couldn't be good news, and sadly, my intuition proved right.

"Cora, it's Mack. You sitting down?" he asked, his voice cutting through the line.

"What now, god dammit?" I pleaded, clutching my head in anticipation.

"Your 'plastic surgeon'—she's gone."

"What are you talking about?"

"Dr. Shore. She was found strangled in her clinic early this morning."

"Huh? How did you…?"

"…thought I wouldn't find out? Your miraculous recovery?"

"Mack, please—" I exhaled, struggling to maintain my composure. "Are you serious? Dr. Shore's dead? Who would…?"

"You know, I was about to ask you the same thing?"

"What the hell does that mean? Look, I need to get access to her work."

"No Cora. What you need to do is back away."

"Mack, you don't understand…"

"I warned you that this was a dangerous game. You need to leave it alone."

"Leave it alone? Do you think this is a hobby? Something to occupy my time? These fuckers murdered my friend, and I'm the only one doing shit about it—I'm not backing away from anything." I shouted, my voice cracking.

"Cora, this goes beyond the Ring. It's a very nasty case you're wrapped up in."

"What do you mean 'this goes beyond the Ring?' …and why was Dr. Shore targeted?"

"Are you listening to me? Shore's gone. And you'll be next. I suggest you run a mile and hope they forget about you. Do understand what I'm saying?"

Emotionally drained, I lacked the strength to argue. I simply hung up the phone, burying my head in my hands. I couldn't believe this was happening. It seemed no matter how hard I tried; I was always a step behind those who sought to keep their activities shrouded.

Mack's words looped in my mind, their implication heavier with each repetition. Could Dr. Shore's death be tied to her classified government work? Or was it her research on the serum? And what did Mack mean when he said this went beyond the Ring? The questions layered on top of each other, all without an answer, compounding my frustration.

Dr. Shore's demise gutted my last hope of possibly reversing the side effects. It felt like someone had pulled the floor out from under, leaving me to freefall with no parachute.

The enemy I faced was sophisticated enough to eliminate her and brazen enough to leave traces meant to be found. Was I stepping into a trap or stumbling upon a conspiracy so expansive it exceeded even Mack's jurisdiction?

***

In the following weeks, my apartment became a fortress of gloom. Curtains shut, lights dimmed. Sleep was a battle between waking reality and nightmares. Food lost its taste; time, a cruel illusion.

Rhea latched onto my weakened state like a leech. "No more breadcrumbs to follow, huh? What's a lab rat to do now?"

With a scream, I knocked everything off the coffee table. "You wanted this!"

"If blaming me is your coping mechanism, go ahead."

My skin became a canvas for self-inflicted wounds, evidence of my desperate need to feel something—anything—other than this. My attempts to claw away at my invasive tattoos only worsened the problem.

"You weren't there for her final moments. That's very sad," said the voice in my head.

I squeezed my eyes shut, hands clamped over my ears. "Stop lying!"

"You failed her." Rhea's words were needles, each one puncturing another hole in my resilience.

Suicidal thoughts tiptoed around the periphery of my mind, yet each time they surfaced, a wisp of stubbornness ignited.

I couldn't allow her to break me. My instinct to resist Rhea was a painstaking process, an uphill battle against an opponent who knew my every weakness, my every fear.

But then I realized, how can I fight fire with fire when the enemy is within?

"Leverage is how you measure one's true allegiance."—my retort to Vincent ran through my subconscious. Then a notion so perverse formed in my head that I hesitated even to articulate it.

"Rhea," I ventured, casting the line but not fully committing. "Do you ever ponder the irony of our existence?" I asked cautiously.

There was an unusual pause from the insistent noise that had long been Rhea's calling card—I had her attention.

"It occurs to me that there's a greater enemy than the one within. If this 'vessel' we're both tethered to is destroyed, neither of us wins. We both disappear. Wouldn't that prove a little… inconvenient to your plans?"

Just as I began to second-guess myself, she responded.

"Irony is a luxury for those who can afford it. What are you getting at?"

"I'm suggesting that we have something in common beyond biology. A need for self-preservation. The people who killed Dr. Shore would certainly come for me next."

Silence. I sensed Rhea's internal war, the clash between her instinct for survival and the antipathy that defined our twisted relationship. Finally, she spoke, her voice dripping with contempt.

"I am Rhea, a force unto myself. And yet, I am bound to your very existence. Separate but connected, like grotesque, conjoined twins. Do you think I relish this base existence? Being stuck without form, squirming like a maggot in your carcass?"

Her voice was sharp and full of bitterness. The candor caught me off guard. I composed myself. "So you understand the paradox?" I asked tentatively.

"Understanding isn't the same as agreement," she fired back. "Your woes are minuscule compared to what I have endured."

I took a deep breath, forcing down the emotional surge her words had ignited. "Alright, you're tormented too. I get it. But consider this, Rhea: we're in a situation where someone's literally trying to kill us—as in, both of us. Fighting each other isn't just petty; it's suicidal."

She seemed to ponder my logic. I imagined her spectral form pacing around my mental chambers, considering, calculating. "Hmph," she finally grunted.

"So you agree?" I asked cautiously.

"Listen here, little sister, none of these 'threats' that you constantly fail to address would even exist if I had form to enact my will upon those insects. There is no pact. No integration. No compromise. You either do as you're told or we both perish, which means Samantha's precious memory will forever be smeared by your incompetence," she said, but I recognized a chink in her armor.

"Yes, perhaps, but you've haunted my soul for long enough for me to realize that your supreme sense of destiny coupled with your... 'winning personality' would never allow you to relinquish your ambitions," I replied.

"Don't fool yourself. This does not make us allies. And as for Mr. Robert Prince, let's get one thing straight. I intend to sever the head from the body and ascend the throne. But his organization will remain, as it will further my own agenda.

To achieve this, there needs to be dysentery among the ranks, and some minor structural damage to aid in the regime change."

"What agenda is that, Rhea?"

"That's none of your concern. We may share the same intellect, but make no mistake, this is my domain, and you will do my bidding as instructed, or I will ensure that you never know a moment's peace until they lay your desecrated corpse alongside Samanthas'—with her death unavenged. Are we clear, little sister?"

Rhea was impossible. Even in the face of mutual destruction, she remained relentless.

"Look, Rhea...."

"Careful...this is not a negotiation," she warned slowly, in a tone I'd not sensed before.

I despised having to acknowledge it, but fear had gripped me. I struggled to reason with my own thoughts, all the while dreading the potential response that would emerge from the twisted confines of my psyche. The creeping sense of madness was overwhelming.

"I just want Prince to pay for what he did—that's all."

"Fine. But let's be clear. As I indulge your ill-fated optimism, did you ever stop to think that I am precisely the being I was designed to be? I am not some fragment to be conveniently reinserted back into obscurity. Your arrogant sense of entitlement is offensive. It is I, Rhea, who will absorb you. Now, we have our 'agreement.'"

After enduring Rhea's impassioned soliloquy, I felt an odd sense of emptiness—a void where normally there would have been anger or defiance. Rhea's presence was undeniable, her influence spreading like a dark stain seeping into my very being.

I clung to the naïve hope that we could coexist, that I could temper her cruelty with reason and mutual self-preservation. But it was obvious to me now - Rhea did not want balance.

She was a ruthless, hostile invader, a parasite feeding off my misery. She sought domination and would shatter my psyche to achieve it.

I had hoped to save us both, to heal the fracture inside me. But some breaks cannot be mended. The revelation crystallized in my thoughts—meeting Rhea's ferocity with compassion was naïve, even reckless. She would exploit any vulnerability as a wedge to gain control. I had to stop clinging to who I was and become who I needed to be.

And so, amidst Rhea's relentless onslaught, a frustrated determination ignited. If she would not be tamed, I would unleash her and tap into the ferocious essence I had tried to suppress.

Controlled mayhem—perhaps the only way to derail her plans for complete domination. By providing her with a taste of the chaos she so desired, maybe—I could find a weakness, a crack in her seemingly impervious facade. Now, with a hostile internal alliance brokered, I was free to focus on establishing myself as a valuable asset to Prince's organization.

Chapter 16
Between Hell and a Hard Place

Vincent eased his black Mercedes into the darkened parking lot, while intense headlights cast a sweeping glow over the rough, uneven brickwork. We came to a halt, with the glow from the dashboard casting an eerie shadow over his face.

"Damien's pleased," he said, flicking the end of his cigarette out the half-open window. Smoke plumed into the air, blending with the scent of worn leather and perfume as I sat, legs crossed beside him.

"He's particularly interested in the last targets you flagged."

I watched the ember at the end of his cigarette glow brighter as he took a drag. "Good," I said, my voice tempered.

He exhaled. "Lila, level with me—how the hell do you pull this kind of intel?"

"I hope you're not asking me to divulge my trade secrets, Vincent?" I replied, attempting to deflect his question.

"I've been around. Shit like this doesn't just fall into your lap-even with the connections we got—full wrap, biometrics, surveillance, affiliations, bank, mobile and internet records, even their damn informant status, which is highly classified I might add—what's the deal, Lila?"

"You have your honey traps, and I have mine," I replied.

His lips twitched into something resembling a smile. "Damien wants you to broaden your scope. He's eyeing several politicians who could assist with a few moves we're planning—once 'persuaded,'" he said, handing me a piece of paper with names scribbled down.

"I'm on it," I replied, sliding the note into my breast pocket.

The car's engine roared to life as he turned the ignition key. "I'm sure you are," he mused, shifting the car into drive and exiting the alley, rejoining the flow of traffic.

***

As the months passed, my existence within Prince's organization became more entrenched. My involvement in manipulating the lives of those we targeted was distasteful, yet an area in which I became highly proficient. Even Damien, a human fortress of cold rationality, began to lean on my insight.

As I sat across from him in his office during a rain-soaked afternoon, he appeared thoughtful, engrossed by the scene beyond his window. Swiveling his chair, he broached the subject of possible expansion for the group's cybercrime division. He navigated a fine line, avoiding self-incrimination while implying that my unique skill set could further the organization's objectives. The subtle tension characterizing our interactions never went unnoticed—he remained guarded, preferring to keep me in his line of sight.

A prudent move, but ultimately ineffective. Unbeknownst to him, each word uttered was being recorded by nano-tech listening devices, sending all gathered intel to a server in a hidden location. My surveillance equipment, discreetly installed throughout the compound, captured every damning word from Vincent and his fellow goons to Damien and the rest of his lieutenants.

I gathered dirt right across the board. Every illegal scheme, every despicable detail, all preserved for posterity. I remained sharp, cataloging vulnerabilities and connections. I subtly steered discussions, eliciting telling reactions. Self-incrimination flourished in the false comfort of their private sanctum. These recordings were just the beginning. I built dossiers detailing their networks of corrupt politicians, law enforcement, and all the major corporations they had dealings with - Vanguard, BlackRock, State Street - all the usual suspects were featured.

The ugly truth took shape, recorded, and documented. My encrypted archive grew into a Pandora's box capable of reducing this evil empire to rubble. Yet Prince remained aloof, insulated by a wall of criminality just beyond my grasp.

While caution tempered my approach, Rhea preferred to shake the hornet's nest and provoke immediate reactions.

With precision that was almost supernatural, she guided my hand as I spun an intricate network of lies and manipulation. Rhea's brilliance shone as she meticulously orchestrated a complex scheme to weaken Damien's authority and solidify our position in the organization.

While Marcus, Prince's Chief Technical Officer, and I were immersed in conversation about how to strengthen the Ring's security, Damien appeared, holding the door ajar.

"Lila, a word," Damien interrupted.

"Certainly," I answered, extricating myself from Marcus with a practiced smile. He took the hint and busied himself analyzing some code on the screen while I stepped out into the corridor to hear Damien's concerns.

"There have been some... irregularities in our recent venture. What do you make of this?" he said, handing me a report.

I glanced over the file before handing it back, meeting his gaze squarely—as Rhea's influence stirred. "Irregularities?

What's the issue?" I asked.

"Senator Klein seems to have reneged on our agreement. Was he not part of your flock?"

"I delivered on my end, as usual, Damien. If there's 'irregularities,' it's downstream."

He took a slow step closer. "Is that so?"

My eyes never leaving him, I continued. "Yes. It seems to me, Damien, that we're navigating through complex terrain. Maybe we should focus on how best to adapt."

A look of credulity crossed his face. "Adapt? To irregularities? Are you feeling OK Lila?"

"Never better, Damien," I replied, struggling to keep Rhea's disdain in check.

"This is on you. I want answers. Get it sorted," he said, pulling rank.

"I got you covered—boss," my words slow and monotone.

He studied me for a prolonged second before abruptly turning on his heel. The terse exchange provoked by Rhea had shifted my once cautious yet amiable relationship with Damien to a realm of suspicion. This sudden pivot ratcheted up my anxiety, leaving me stranded between his newfound skepticism and Rhea's redirected fury. This brief respite from the internal hostility felt as if a dark fog had momentarily receded, only to reveal gathering storm clouds in the distance.

***

As the weeks unfolded, the air grew heavy, each glance exchanged between Damien and I carried an increasing weight of unspoken tension.

Powerless to diffuse the brewing animosity, I bided my time as Rhea's dutiful host and played my part without protest.

Provided with free rein, Rhea was eager to seize the initiative. Opting for an indirect assault, she embedded false intel within the Ring's orbit, hinting at a lucrative illegal shipment bound for the port. An anonymous tip to the authorities guaranteed a raid.

Unaware of Rhea's machinations, Damien dispatched his most loyal enforcers to secure the supposed loot. Yet, behind the scenes, Rhea had tipped off a rival gang as well, sparking a brutal clash between Damien's men, the police, and the rivals.

Damien snatched up his phone as it buzzed on his desk.

"Boss, we got a problem!" reported Alex, one of his enforcers.

Damien's grip tightened as he pressed the microphone to his lips. "Explain."

"We're not the only ones here. Someone tipped off another crew. And the cops. We're in bad shape!"

The backdrop of gunfire and shouting lent terrifying credibility to Alex's words.

"Secure the shipment and pull out. Now."

"There's fuck-all here. It's a setup!"

"SHIT. Pull back," Damien instructed.

More gun shots rang out before the line went silent, then echoed static. Damien yelled into the phone, "Alex? Alex!" but it was futile. The violent showdown had eliminated his entire team, with the shipment nowhere to be found. Meanwhile, we cunningly remained at a safe distance, untouched by suspicion.

In the aftermath, Damien grappled with the fallout of a disastrously failed operation, his once unshakable standing within the organization tainted. A fleeting pang of sympathy arose, knowing all too well the grim fate that awaited those who wandered into Rhea's cross-hairs.

As I entertained the thought, I sensed the air thicken around me, and prepared myself for her next audacious gambit—one that would surely stretch my ethical boundaries to breaking point.

Chapter 17
Unleashed

With the path now clear, Rhea's zeal surged. In no time at all, she had marked her next target within the organization. Charlotte Garcia, an illicit art dealer and a close associate of Damien.

Garcia's role in laundering millions for the Ring made her a key figure. Sabotaging her would not only destabilize operations but also furnish irrefutable proof of financial crimes—evidence I could use against Prince. Rhea remained the wildcard, but considering the increased scrutiny we were under, even she would likely see the wisdom in a more nuanced approach.

Arriving at her private art studio located downtown, we met under the guise of discussing prospective buyers for her latest collection. Charlotte greeted me as the heavy door closed behind us, sealing off the studio from the city's noise. "Lila, it's good to see you. Let me give you a tour."

"I'd love that. You always find the most... intriguing pieces," I replied.

We wandered through the studio, an assortment of oil on canvas and sculptures. The air smelled of fresh paint and old money.

Pausing in front of a modernist piece, Charlotte glanced my way. "This one's causing quite a buzz among private collectors."

"Of course, it has that provocative flair you're so adept at marketing," I said.

"Well, one must know her audience," she replied with a courteous smile.

We continued our conversation, delving into potential buyers, logistical challenges, and terms that would benefit both parties. All the while, a listening device concealed in the clasp of my bracelet captured every incriminating word.

"I must say, some of these pieces have an unsettling aura. Almost as if they're yearning to break free from their canvas." The words rolled off my tongue, and yet felt foreign.

Charlotte looked slightly taken aback. "That's one way to put it. Art often reflects the most hidden parts of ourselves, doesn't it?"

"Indeed, and some parts are best left hidden, wouldn't you agree?"

Charlotte smiled nervously. "Of course. Discretion is an art form in itself."

"Ah, but how long can art truly be contained? Eventually, it finds a way to free itself, to shatter its restraints. Wouldn't you say?" My words punctuated the air like a well-placed brushstroke as Charlotte stood puzzled.

Then I felt an unbidden chill creep over me as I witnessed my own reflection take on a menacing hue. My eyes, hollow and stripped of all compassion, locked onto hers. Confusion played across her face as she sensed something amiss. But before Charlotte could articulate her alarm, the façade of my usual friendly self snapped back into place.

"And what do we have here?" I said gesturing towards a piece that stood alone.

"Are you OK?" Charlotte enquired timidly, unable to shake off of what she had just witnessed.

"Am I OK? It's you who seems a bit off, babe," I responded.

Charlotte flashed a forced smile, turning away to unwrap the centerpiece of her collection. But it was too late. Rhea's predatory instincts were triggered, and my heart thundered in my chest as I watched my hand remove a long hairpin from my neatly tied bun. Her intent was clear, her resolve chilling. I was paralyzed, a spectator to my own monstrous act, as I thrust the pin into Charlotte's spine with a muted thud.

Her legs buckled, sending her stumbling toward a priceless artwork for support. But her grip failed her, and she collapsed into a disorganized heap of boxes, her eyes pleading for mercy.

"No one will hear you," Rhea's voice whispered in Charlotte's ear. I watched, simultaneously trapped within my own body. The life in her face dimmed until only the cold void of death remained.

"You can't possibly believe you're any sort of angel after this," Rhea's voice intruded, the tone barbed and coarse.

"Oh my god. You're insane. I didn't want her dead." I said, struggling to keep my voice low.

"You needed me to do what you couldn't. To carry out your dirty work while you play innocent," Rhea cooed, mockery lacing every syllable.

"This isn't about senseless killing. She was divulging exactly what I needed to know."

"What do you think the end game is here Lila? Do you expect to see Prince hauled off to prison?"

"I want justice for Sam! I didn't allow you to intervene for this monstrosity!"

"Allow me? Rhea's voice erupted. "Listen here Lila, you don't allow anything. The only reason you're not hunched over in a ball reliving those terrible nightmares and blackouts is because I deem it so."

"Well, do it then—see how far your grand schemes get without me."

"Pathetic! You say you're doing this for Samantha, but deep down, it's to quench your own thirst for significance," Rhea sneered.

Her words struck a nerve. "That's not true."

"Isn't it? Then why 'allow' me to do what you're too cowardly to do? Face it, 'Cora', without me, Damien, Prince, and the rest of these maggots would eat you alive, and then ravage your corpse."

"Maybe so, but you need me just as much as I need you—and killing Charlotte was not some evil genius plan to punish Damien—you wanted to satisfy your lust for blood."

"Can't a girl enjoy her work?" Rhea quipped.

My silent scream tore through me. It was a blend of frustration and despair, a manifestation of the internal war I couldn't afford to wage while also fighting the Ring.

"Cathartic, isn't it?" Rhea continued.

I clutched my head. The mental anguish threatened to split my skull in two. Then, I felt my phone vibrating in my pocket, jolting me. Damien. His name lit up the screen. My pulse quickened. I shot a glance at Charlotte's lifeless form, then back at the phone. Why call now? Was he onto me? My mind raced. Should I answer or avoid and play for time?

"Pick it up, Lila," Rhea barked.

She had a point. Ignoring the call would only raise suspicion. If Damien was tracking me, the jig was up anyway.

I pushed the button. "Damien, what's up?" I said, steadying my voice.

"Where are you?" His tone was direct, almost curt.

"At home, digging into the senator case, like you wanted. What do you need?"

"The 'big guy' wants to see you. Tomorrow, 10 a.m., sharp."

"You mean—"

"Don't say his name. Not on the phone."

"…Erm, OK. What's it about?" I said, trying to feel him out.

"He wants to meet his newest rising star."

"Alright, I'll be there."

"And Lila," he paused, "don't fuck this up."

The call ended, and Rhea's voice wormed its way back into my consciousness.

"Ah, an audience with the 'Prince.' How delightful. Just don't show up quivering and spluttering all over the place."

"I can handle Prince on my own—I didn't get this far by 'quivering and spluttering,'—did I, Rhea?"

"What do you want? A cookie? Listen up—the goal is to have Prince so trusting he never sees it coming."

"We're aligned then. I want him to pay; you want him dead. Either outcome suits me."

"Finally thinking like a grown-up. I'm impressed. Now, handle Charlotte's mess, and let's move."

Rhea's mockery aside, the meeting unsettled me. Damien was a shrewd operator. Was this a setup? Had he pieced together my double dealings? The botched shipment deal? Maybe he'd found my surveillance tech? Or was this the break I'd been waiting for—the chance to take Prince down?

I exhaled, my gaze lingering on Charlotte's lifeless form. I had to push forward, risks and all, Rhea be damned. This was the juncture, the point of no return, and I was all in.

Chapter 18
A Royal Invitation

I prowled back and forth like a caged animal in my living room. In less than an hour, I'd be face to face with Robert Prince, scrutinized by the very man responsible for Sam's demise.

He would assess me, probing for any weakness or inconsistency. One misstep could undo everything. Rhea, ever-present, would prove to be a help or a hindrance depending on whether our objectives truly aligned. But she was an entity unto herself and there was no time for second-guessing.

Turning to the bed, my outfit lay neatly folded. It was a carefully curated look—feminine but formidable. I had selected tight black leather pants, a fitted blazer, sleek pointed ankle boots, and a burgundy shirt cut low enough to suggest allure but not expose vulnerability. Dark makeup would project intensity while long jet-black hair tied in a ponytail would highlight my sharp features. This had to be a temptress outfit for the mind, more so than the body—although both served a purpose.

I dressed methodically, straightening each item until it aligned with my vision. As I applied the final touches, the figure staring back from the mirror exuded confidence laced with cold efficiency.

My pulse was still deafening, my nerves on edge. Today decided whether I ascended the ranks or met a grim end.

With a final glance, I inhaled deeply. "I'm ready," I whispered to my reflection, a face that now felt like my own.

"Don't fuck it up, little sister," said the voice, timely as ever.

I turned and headed for the door, slamming it shut behind me, and set off to attend Prince's court.

***

The heavily fortified gates of the compound loomed larger than usual. Though I'd been here many times before, today was different. The guards flanking the entrance watched me closely, fingers resting casually near holstered guns, despite having waved me through numerous times.

"Got to frisk you, Thompson," orders from…." he said, gesturing upwards with a gloved finger.

"Do what you have to do, Max," I replied. "It's business."

He nodded to his partner, who stepped forward. "Arms out," he said.

I complied with the brisk search.

"She's clean." Satisfied he'd followed orders, he waved me through.

A door at the top of the marble staircase led me to a secluded elevator guarded by a hulk of a man. He knew of me, but we'd not had dealings.

"Miss," he acknowledged with a discreet nod.

"Benny," I replied, returning the courtesy.

"Got Thompson here for Mr. P," he voiced into his cufflink. The clipped response, "Send her up," buzzed from his waist.

"Damien will escort you once at the top," he said, swiping his key card and stepping aside. I entered and turned to face him as the doors slid closed, sealing me in.

Upon reopening, Damien stood waiting, an imposing figure, as always, in his sharply tailored suit.

"Lila, follow me," he instructed, ushering me down a corridor lined with statues that appeared as warriors frozen in a timeless skirmish. We stopped outside large ornate double doors flanked by two heavily armed guards. They eyed me with muted interest. Damien knocked, pushed open, and stood aside. "Sir. Ms. Thompson," he announced.

"You can go in," he said, before gently pulling the door shut behind me.

***

Prince sat behind a large desk of dark, polished wood, its surface almost entirely clear except for a few strategically placed files and a sleek laptop. He was a study in calculated elegance, clothed in a charcoal suit so finely tailored it seemed to meld with him. His tie was a muted silver, and his cufflinks caught the light, glinting briefly as he moved.

As I laid eyes on him for the first time, a wave of emotion surged, nearly overwhelming my senses. Memories of Sam flooded back—her laughter, her kindness, the light she brought to my life—and then the crushing weight of her absence. Rage simmered, and my heart pounded, each beat a reminder of why I had infiltrated this man's empire.

The walls were adorned with art that was both modern and unsettling, images that seemed to glare at me from all angles. Adjacent to the artwork, a large gun cabinet commanded attention. Encased in reinforced glass and framed in matte black steel—a tactical masterpiece.

Rows of firearms from sleek handguns to formidable assault rifles were meticulously arranged, each in its custom-fitted slot. The cabinet was more than a display; it was a statement of power and violence.

I took a deep breath, forcing the memories back into the steel box I'd locked them in. My face remained impassive, my posture upright. I couldn't allow another slip. The stakes were far too high.

"Lila Thompson," he said, his voice a low rumble that filled the room. He observed my presence for a moment, taking in my attire, my figure, and the calculated confidence I projected. There was a brief acknowledgment of the woman before him. But it was gone as quickly as it appeared, replaced by dead eyes that gave nothing away.

"Please," he said, gesturing towards an antique leather chair.

"Your work has caught my attention." His words were complimentary but guarded.

"Thank you," I replied, matching his tone.

"You've made an impression, I see," he remarked. "To what end, I wonder?"

There it was, the blunt question hidden beneath pleasantries, aimed right at my motives.

"I believe the goals of the organization align with my own. The more value I add, the more I receive in return. It's good business." A safe response, aligning our interests while revealing a plausible motive.

Prince skimmed through my records, his eyes darting over the pages before tossing it casually onto his desk. "Files never give the full picture, do they?" he said, looking up.

"So, Ms. Thompson, explain to me how a Stanford-educated rich girl ends up in the company of men like Vincent Russo and Damien Black. You clearly don't need the money."

I leaned back in my chair, crossed my legs, and measured my response carefully. "Money isn't the only form of power, Mr. Prince. And power is a currency that interests me greatly."

He raised an eyebrow, intrigued but cautious. "Go on."

"Growing up the way I did, bouncing from one foster home to another, taught me something crucial. Stability is an illusion. The only real security lies in the ability to adapt, to manipulate your surroundings to your advantage."

Prince nodded. "…and your charity work, your political donations—what advantage do they bring you?"

"Connections, influence, a seat at the table," I said, my voice smoldering with dark intentions. "My charity work isn't philanthropy; it's strategy. It opens doors that money alone can't. As for my criminal record, well, sometimes you have to break a few laws to make new ones."

"I see. And what does Ms. Thompson want—big picture?" he asked, probing.

"To gather enough power so that I never have to rely on anyone but myself."

Prince reclined. "A lofty goal. But even the most powerful people have vulnerabilities."

"True," I conceded. "But the trick is not to eliminate your vulnerabilities; it's to make them so costly to exploit that no one would dare try."

A knowing smirk crept across his face. "Well, Ms. Thompson, I appreciate your candor."

"As I appreciate yours, Mr. Prince," I replied, sensing the mutual respect that had formed between us.

"Your work with Vincent has proven to be lucrative—he speaks highly of you. And the business with Damien, despite recent 'irregularities,' has also proven to be fruitful."

I detected a note of veiled critique in his words. "Mr. Prince, we operate in a volatile industry. Irregularities aren't exceptions; they're expectations. My job is to turn those into opportunities. My commitment to the organization is unwavering."

The mood in the room shifted as Prince sat back, fingers steepled in consideration.

"You have proven yourself quite capable, Ms. Thompson. More so than many who have served far longer."

Prince continued. "Effective immediately, you'll be responsible for our high-level target acquisitions. A role critical to our endeavors—and one well suited to your particular skill set."

My breath caught imperceptibly. He was offering an elevated position that granted immense access while aligning me more closely under his direct oversight. This was the opportunity I'd been waiting for. The chance to link him personally to a criminal conspiracy and expose the whole organization in the process.

"I'm flattered. I certainly look forward to delivering."

Prince regarded me for a long moment before speaking again.

"Let's be clear. This is not blind faith on my part. You will be under

Damien's command, but you'll report to me as well. You'll find I keep a close watch regarding matters of such a delicate nature."

We both understood the implications. This was a test, one I could not afford to fail. The stakes were high, but so too was the opportunity to finally bring Sam's killer to justice.

"I understand the gravity of this responsibility, Mr. Prince. You won't be disappointed."

"Good," he replied, before gesturing toward the large doors in dismissal.

As I left his office, I felt the magnitude of what had just transpired. I was now a key figure in a vast criminal enterprise, holding a position that offered both peril and promise. The objective was clear: gather damning evidence, and mount a case.

But the path was fraught with obstacles. Damien's suspicion remained a constant variable I had to manage—especially with Charlotte's disappearance, which he had yet to mention.

And, of course, there was Rhea, my covert adversary, who possessed a craftiness that defied prediction. Her plots were a hidden dimension, a spectral world where her schemes were formless and disconnected from my own. I'd have to channel her ferocity while preventing it from exploding in ways that could jeopardize the mission.

And all the while, I'd have to continue to solidify my reputation, not just as a competent operative, but as a formidable one. I needed to be the person everyone, including Prince, believed could get the impossible done. Only then would I have the access and trust to dismantle their operation from within like a poison pill.

I stepped into the elevator and met my reflection in its mirrored walls—a stranger wearing a familiar face. Gripping the rails, I felt the velvet cage descend. In my mind, gears seemed to shift, grinding toward a singular purpose with each floor passed.

The doors slid open as I reached the ground floor. Benny, the muscular guard, stood aside, parting my exit with a stern nod. "Thompson," he acknowledged.

"Thank you," I replied.

I caught Max's attention on my way past security.

"Good night Ms. Thompson," he said, glancing up from his monitors before pressing the button to release the electric gate.

"Indeed, Max—indeed," I replied softly, a battle cry filled with steely resolve.

I stepped out beyond the compound, absorbed by the cold night—every stride distancing me from my past, hurtling me toward the unknown.

Chapter 19
Hostile Takeover

Elevated to my new role, I channeled my energies with ruthless precision. The criteria were set: high-value assets, from lawmakers to CEOs. The method, honed and perfected, was executed with ruthless efficiency: honey traps leading to blackmail. Each day was a deluge of classified intelligence, my eyes combing through the spoils from the FBI's vaults to isolate the most susceptible targets.

Those individuals with a proclivity for engaging in illicit acts with minors were top of the list. The explicit material we gathered turned my stomach, but the evidence against Prince and his organization continued to mount.

My reports were comprehensive, detailing not just the operation but also the network of political corruption and sadistic depravity. An unending stream of young boys and girls harvested from foster homes, youth facilities, and shelters, all delivered into the hands of predators as bait to ensnare other predators.

After months of Machiavellian maneuvering, my influence had grown immeasurable. My keen insights, bolstered by Rhea's 'talents', made me a linchpin in their ranks. However, despite these inroads, Prince remained adept at shielding himself from direct incrimination.

Eager to seize the moment, I engineered a sophisticated ruse. I would present an ambitious plan for global expansion, that would allow me to build a case with Prince's fingerprints all over it. Even with all his political connections, once the evidence was released to the public, he'd be a huge liability the authorities could not ignore.

***

On a wet and overcast afternoon, with Prince's blessing, I convened a meeting in the conference room. It brimmed with the upper echelon of the organization's top-ranking members, each a ruthless criminal in their own right—including Damien. Hues of black, brown, and blood red adorned the walls of the chamber. A high-tech security panel embedded in the large polished mahogany table served as a stark reminder: this was a place for strategy and serious endeavors, not idle chatter.

As the ambient noise quieted, I sensed the "other" stir within. It was a subtle but absolute possession, entombing me with an icy chill while I still drew breath. The Lila, who avoided confrontation, was supplanted by Rhea who thrived on it. My steps resonated with authority, silencing the room as I approached. The air cloyed with intrigue and expectation as Rhea took center stage.

"Gentlemen," she began, her voice laced with gravitas, "I have a proposition that I believe merits your attention." She assessed the line-up of hardened faces for signs of resistance before unfurling our vision. One that promised not merely to extend, but to entrench the organization on an international stage.

It was a hostile takeover in all but name, and predictably, it was met with strong resistance.

Damien was the first to challenge. "This is a reckless venture. We risk exposure, and for what?"

"More profit, more power," Rhea replied. "The complacency within our ranks stagnates growth. It's time for change."

"Easy to say when you're not the one putting your neck on the line," another member said.

"Who the fuck does she think she is?" another member shot back.

"The same person who delivered when you were jammed up, Andrew. Let's stick to the topic." Then I felt it, a shift within me—Rhea had already marked his card.

"Settle down Drew," Prince interjected, observing the heated discussion.

"I agree with Damien," another member added. "This plan might backfire."

"My plans don't backfire," Rhea countered.

"Fortune favors the bold Mr. Black," she said, throwing her words squarely in Damien's direction.

Whispers circulated and tension mounted.

"Enough!" Prince's voice cut through the noise. The talk dissipated, every face turned towards him, some with relief, others with apprehension. His tone was measured, imbued with authority that commanded respect.

"Damien, I understand your reservations—I share them too. But I also see merit in Lila's proposal. We have become complacent. We need innovation to grow."

"Gentlemen, I'm sure there are other matters that require your attention. We'll reconvene. You're dismissed."

"Lila, wait outside," he said, followed by "Damien, a quick word."

The room was still for a moment, and then slowly, the members dispersed through the large double doors.

Damien's eyes fixed on me as I trailed the men outside. "This is not a game, Lila," he said as she passed.

"I'm fully aware, Damien, and I'm deadly serious," I replied, the irony of my words eluding him. With that said, I felt her presence subside, retreating to her usual haunt, in the shadows, omnipresent.

Left to calm the flames fanned by Rhea, the gravity of the situation weighed on me. Every tribulation endured had distilled into this very moment. Yet, conversations whispered in seclusion loomed as a potential unraveling of all I had worked for. Could Damien be planting seeds of dissent in Prince's mind? Had he unearthed damning evidence of my plans? But to indulge in fear or hesitation was a luxury I couldn't afford.

Suddenly, the doors swung open with a gust as Damien exited.

"He wants you…" he said through gritted teeth before disappearing down the hallway.

I straightened my tailored jacket, inhaled deeply, and pushed the double door apart as I entered.

I glanced at Prince sitting at the opposite end of the heavy table. I approached without hesitation.

"Lila, take a seat. Continue."

I repositioned one of the heavily studded leather chairs to face him. "What I'm talking about is full control," I began. "Merchandise, transportation, safe houses, the operatives—all the moving pieces consolidated on a global scale."

"…I understand the potential, Lila," he said, cutting me off abruptly. "But centralization comes with significant liability—that concerns me."

"That can be mitigated. And the upside is monumental," I replied.

"Since your promotion, you've consistently exceeded expectations.

But this proposal—I don't grant that level of operational freedom lightly. Especially to a relative newcomer with grand designs on my enterprise."

"Seems like Damien had a few choice words to share," I observed.

Prince surged to his feet, his hands planted firmly on the polished table. "That man has done more for me than I care to mention. You'll do well to keep him onside. Your ascent would have been unfeasible without his implicit endorsement."

"I hold Damien in high regard and appreciate the opportunity I've been given. However, sentimentality has never been my guiding principle."

"Let me enlighten you, Ms. Thompson," Prince said, straightening his posture while slowly pacing back and forth. "This empire wasn't built on sentimentality. It was built on choices so dark, they'd make you question your own humanity."

He paused, allowing his words to percolate. "I've been through the trenches, seen men buckle under the weight of their own decisions. I've ordered hits on friends, betrayed mentors, and orchestrated the downfall of those far more powerful than you can imagine. I've watched as their empires crumble, lives and families ruined, all to build this—what you see before you."

He stopped pacing and turned toward me. "I've made deals with devils, crossed lines you wouldn't dare approach. I've stained my hands so thoroughly that if I had a soul, it would have long since been forfeited. And Damien? He was right there beside me, making those same choices, crossing those same lines."

Prince now stood peering down at me, only inches away from my face. "Do you understand now, Lila, the type of men you are in business with? Do you understand where this path leads?"

I instinctively pulled back, yet maintained my composure. "I understand perfectly, Prince. And if I were concerned with eternal damnation, I'd have opted for a very different career path."

He smirked, taking a second to regard me. "How do I know you're not just another temptress looking to hitch your wagon to my star?"

"Track records don't lie. Besides, I'm a star in my own right, Prince."

"Hum," he said, backing away like a posturing gorilla having assessed my authenticity.

Returning to his desk, he reclined in his high-backed leather chair—a throne in a den that was an extension of his calculated personality.

Releasing my breath, I sized up my surroundings that had morphed into our gladiatorial arena. The walls were a gallery of conquests. Stuffed animals with lifeless eyes seemed to confer a savage legitimacy upon him. Meanwhile, a bookshelf stacked with heavy volumes on economics, psychology, geopolitics, and military history divulged another dimension to his character.

"And these locations you propose we expand into," he continued. "That's a pretty extensive terrain to conquer. How could you possibly guarantee this will work?

I could see him wrestling with the dichotomy of distrust and opportunity.

"Don't lose him, little sister," came the taunt from within. I ignored her and continued.

"A bold move, yes, with no guarantees. However, the plan is solid, and the timing is right."

He leaned forward, elbows on the table, hands clasped, as if drawing me into his sphere.

"Bold moves are also the riskiest," he retorted. "This level of expansion would make us vulnerable, stretched thin. And then there's you—a recent addition, yet plotting like you're a lifetime member of this organization."

His tone intensified. "Tell me, Lila, why should I grant you such an opportunity?"

"Look, I don't fault your caution, Prince. In your shoes, I'd do the same. The risk is baked in—no doubt, but so too is the reward. We could continue to grow incrementally and let the competition close in—"

I paused. "Or we could seize the initiative. With your leadership and my planning, we could steamroll the entire political class—like the parasites they are. As for being new to the organization—I have proven myself quite capable… 'More so than many who have served far longer'—respectfully, Mr. Prince."

His expression remained neutral, but I saw something—perhaps intrigue, or maybe admiration.

"As for betrayal," I continued, "Let's be blunt: that would ruin us both. And I'm not keen on self-destruction."

Prince hesitated, his gaze drifting to the walls of his office—finally, his eyes returned to me, as if coming to a hard-fought decision.

"Betray me, Lila, make a mockery of this, and all who you hold dear will be held accountable. No exceptions."

"And if you decline, Prince," I responded, "you'll regret it for the rest of your life. It's the path forward, and I trust you see that."

"Very well. Lay the groundwork," he said cautiously. "But understand—I'll be watching you."

"I get it," I replied, a touch of irritation creeping in. "Every action has consequences. I'm aware."

He leaned back, lighting a long cigar. "Good," he exhaled, plumes of smoke wafting in unison with each word. "You may go."

I acknowledged his dismissal with a nod and strode toward the door. Before stepping out, a fleeting glance over my shoulder revealed his eyes scanning every inch of my figure—a combination of base desire, tempered with caution. My gut churned at the thought, yet this was another weapon to be wielded judiciously.

As I pulled the door shut behind me, the air shifted from tension to introspection. Walking down the lonely corridor, Sam's face appeared—an apparition from another era.

Justice was an ever-complicating endeavor that had kicked all this into gear. Yet it wasn't just a single objective. My motives were complex, weighted by varying degrees of guilt, regret, duty, and the harrowing realization that I had evolved, far removed from the woman she once knew.

Among a cadre of killers, I found my place, never so much as a flinch betraying me. I weighed the anatomy of fear against the looming question: What demarcation remained between valor and monstrosity? Would the Sam of yesteryears find pride or disgrace in this new incarnation? A pale vixen with emerald eyes, possessed of a psyche rewritten by inner demons, engulfed by spiraling ink etched into her very DNA.

Was Rhea's prophetic insight accurate? As my moral compass faltered, the seductive allure of power beckoned. Yet, despite the traumas already endured, I sensed that a steeper debt remained to be paid—and Rhea would be its harbinger.

Prince's ignorance of my true objective remained my only saving grace. Behind a smokescreen of greed and ambition, lay a paper trail, tying his empire to a nefarious network of global trafficking and compromised government officials.

I stood on the brink of not merely obliterating his empire but dismantling the cancerous political scaffolding that supported it. My crusade had evolved into something far beyond a personal vendetta—it was a surgical strike aimed at the very heart of the corruption eroding our society.

But complications loomed. Rhea's antagonistic approach to Damien risked waking a sleeping bear, only to provoke the wrath of the demon within. Whether he unraveled my underlying motives or became another casualty of Rhea's blood lust, either outcome would spell disaster for my intricate plans. The grim fact: My path forward was a minefield, growing more perilous with each decision.

Chapter 20
Fractured Alliance

In the days that followed my encounter with Prince, my apartment morphed into a hub of insurgency. With caffeine as my loyal consort, I siphoned through lines of code on my laptop, piecing together the components needed to expose his criminal activities.

Dressed in my go-to uniform—comfortable combat pants and a worn hoodie—I was in my element. My fingers raced, honed with muscle memory and enhanced by the serum. I hacked into various banks and financial institutions with ease. Offshore accounts materialized, their records littered with Prince's fingerprints. I located emails from politicians complicit in his crimes, each thread adding weight to the allegations.

Then came the shipping manifests, shining a light on his secret smuggling ring used to ferry children into a life of abuse. The data sprawled across multiple screens forming an intricate network, each node a damning piece of evidence against him. My phone buzzed in the background, half hidden under a disheveled stack of notes. Without breaking rhythm, I wedged it between my shoulder and ear, answering as I continued my flurry of activity.

"Cora, it's me."

I recognized the gravelly voice. "Hey Mack, What's up?" My tone was distant, betraying my divided attention.

"Are you busy? This isn't really a conversation for the phone. We need to meet."

"Yeah, sure. Where and when?" My cursor blinked impatiently on the screen as if urging me to refocus.

"How about the café, 6 P.M.?"

"Today?"

"Yes, Cora, today."

"Um, Ok. Sure. See you then." I barely registered the end of the call as I hung up, keen to revert to the mission at hand.

***

A few hours later, true to my word, I burst through the café doors, the city's din briefly filling the room behind me. Against the wall sat Mack, his expression appeared grim. For some reason, I felt Rhea stir.

"Cora," Mack said, his voice concerned but firm, "You're spiraling. I've been through the evidence; I know what you've been up to."

I slid into my chair, eager to address his concerns, but it was Rhea who interjected, her voice biting and cold, "Detective, you don't understand the half of it."

His brows furrowed. "What did you say?"

I took a breath, steeling myself to maintain some semblance of normalcy.

"Mack, let's not complicate this, okay? I have things under control."

He shot me a scrutinizing look. "Really? Who's Lila?"

Keeping my face as impassive as possible, I responded, "Lila is a necessity. She's the key to getting close to Prince and dismantling everything he's built."

"By pretending to be someone you're not, and lying to federal agencies? Do you know what you've gotten yourself into?"

He leaned in, his voice dropping a notch. "…and how the hell did you hack the damn FBI? Are you insane?"

"You've been spying on me, haven't you?"

"Absolutely," he replied.

"Well then, you already know I'm not insane. I've infiltrated Prince's organization at every level, something your department couldn't even dream of."

He sighed, shaking his head. "Cora, you've embedded yourself so deep that you can't see a way out. What's the endgame here?"

I leaned back, considering the weight of his words. "…justice for Sam. The end justifies the means."

"That's a slippery slope, and you know it." He paused, sensing he had reached a dead-end with that line of conversation.

"You seem…different, Cora. Are you ok? …and those tattoos, are they new? Covering half your face in tribal markings is a cry for help if ever I saw one."

"What do you have against tattoos? They're really growing on me." I said with a wink.

My internal voice was clear and resolute, but what emerged from my mouth was laced with Rhea's rhetoric. My stomach clenched. I could see Mack's eyes scanning me, trying to grasp what was eluding him.

He leaned forward, concern overtaking his frustration. "Cora, is there something you need to tell me? If so, now is the time."

"You know, it's fascinating what you can accomplish when there's no one else to rely on," I said.

"What the hell does that mean? Do you think I don't want to see Prince's empire fall just as much as you? Do you know the amount of suffering I've witnessed because of that animal?"

"I get it, your hands are tied, good thing mine aren't, ay detective!" Rhea said, twisting the knife further.

"Cora, listen closely. I've overlooked your unofficial 'investigations' because I believe you could do some good, and I sympathize with your loss, but the law is the law, and if you break it, there are consequences - don't put me in that position."

"Fear not, detective, we're on the same team, practically working together... remember?" Rhea said, her veiled threat resounding loud and clear.

Inside, I was frantic, filled with anguish at standing by as Rhea shredded the character of someone trying to rescue the last remnants of my humanity.

The air grew tense as the situation unraveled, Mack's frustration rising, his voice taking on an edge. "OK 'Lila,' so that's how you want to play?"

Rhea taunted Mack even further as I stood postured and defiant. "I tire of this conversation. I don't need you or anyone else, detective. Prince and his organization will fall, and Sam's death will be vindicated. So, either arrest me or stay out of my way."

With that, I turned on my heels, leaving behind a baffled and concerned Mack. As I moved away, Rhea's satisfied purr resonated in my ears, her delight at driving a wedge between Mack and me all too apparent. The weight of the conversation bore down on me. Mack's genuine concern was a touching respite, yet the entity that was Rhea was a puzzle he couldn't piece together.

I embraced the somber night as I walked the 4 blocks home. Mack's words still echoed in my mind, a raft of compassion in a cesspit of treachery. And now, because of Rhea's influence, he found himself entangled in a dangerous conspiracy that could ruin his reputation, his career, or worse.

***

Back in my darkened apartment, the room seemed to tighten around me, walls inching closer like an inhospitable cocoon. Rhea's mocking voice festered in my mind. "Look at you, crushed by sentimentality. He's a fool, and you're weak for caring."

Her words ignited a spark of defiance in me. "Mack doesn't deserve your cruelty. He was trying to help us."

"Us? Don't get it confused little sister. I'm not some wounded part of you to be saved."

I shook my head, trying to silence her, but she continued to taunt me, like a chilling draft seeping through the window frame.

"Mack represents everything holding you back. Your pathetic past, your worthless ties to humanity. These useless eaters would be nothing without someone like me to rule them.... perhaps we should pay Mack a little visit—what do you say, Lila?"

I erupted in a fit of blind panic and rage. "If you touch him, I'll make sure when this is over, you have no 'vessel' to possess, and no 'body' to consume. All your illusions of grandeur will be lost to the ether, sending you back to the pit you crawled out of—you sick fucker."

"Ahhh, there she is—little sister. Finally, some backbone. I'm proud of you. Don't worry, if I wanted Mack dead, he'd be dead. But know this: if he meddles in my affairs, you'll awaken with blood on your hands, and his lifeless body beneath your feet—and don't threaten me ever again, you'll upset me."

And with that, we had a stalemate. I had played my trump card, the only leverage I had over her. Sensing Rhea's hostility simmer beneath the surface, I fell silent. I couldn't deny that her ruthless efficiency had accelerated my plans to bring Prince's organization down. But I had to remain steadfast until I had accomplished my mission. As for my fate, that was an unknown.

Chapter 21
The Mad Prince

Keenly aware of Rhea's wiles, I'd taken the liberty of installing a signal interceptor in Prince's den during our last meeting. This vantage point was a crucial element for cementing my plan to corner him.

As I watched the live feed on my laptop, I witnessed Prince's veneer of stoic resolve falter. The self-control he usually maintained cracked as fists slammed on tables and glass lay shattered on the floor.

I leaned in, adjusting the volume to eavesdrop on the source of his agitation. What had triggered this display of raw emotion?

"Those child-fiddling bastards think they can just shirk their obligations," he sneered, as his assistant stumbled through updates about weakening political alliances.

"Where the fuck is this shit coming from?" he said, pondering the reason for this sudden boldness.

A low thud resonated from the double doors. "Come," Prince commanded.

Michael, one of Prince's minions, appeared. "Boss, we've got a problem," he announced, his voice hesitant.

Prince paused, composing himself. "Go on..."

"I've been informed that some of our corporate partners are 'fluctuating'"

"Straighten your tongue, man."

"Shifting allegiances, sir."

"At this point?" Prince said. "They've clearly forgotten who they're dealing with—perhaps it's time to remind them."

"I'm not sure, boss. It's like we're being outflanked—somehow," he replied.

"Hum. It would seem so. We need to figure out who's moving against us before we start chopping off heads," Prince said.

As they considered strategies to uncover the source of their recent misfortune, the doors burst open again without a knock.

"What now?" Prince snapped, twisting his chair to face the intruder.

"The dock's hot, boss. Feds are all over it. Arrests, impounded shipments—the whole nine yards. Our inside guy says he's compromised," informed Leo, a portly figure of a man.

"Fuck," Prince slammed his hand on the desk.

"Leo, get hold of our guy at the bureau and find out why the hell those Boy Scouts are interfering with my business," Prince said.

"Understood, boss," he confirmed, with sweat still dripping from his brow as he caught his breath.

Prince composed himself. "Appearing vulnerable isn't an option. Fix this Fed problem."

"I'll get my guys on it right away," Leo said.

Prince decreed. "Whatever it takes. I want this under control."

Leo and Michael left, both wearing masks of forced composure. The phone on Prince's desk rang out as he quickly snatched it up.

"Speak," he commanded, his tone as icy as ever.

A brief silence followed as the other party relayed information.

"Your forces are useless! Get control of Richardson's lackeys before they infest everything - unless you want bodies littering the streets!"

The police chief's excuses and attempts to explain the rival gang's sudden encroachment only stoked Prince's fury.

"Need I remind you of your precarious position regarding certain underaged individuals? I'm not asking for a favor. Get this sorted."

Prince slammed down the phone. He knew something had destabilized the long-standing truce between rival organizations, but he was busy fighting fires at home.

The door creaked open again as Prince's accountant entered, clutching a bundle of papers. "Sir, I'm afraid we have an issue..."

Before he could finish, Prince snatched the documents. His eyes widened in disbelief as he scanned the damning financial reports. In an explosion of uncontrolled fury, he swept everything off his desk.

"What the fuck is this?" he bellowed, turning his rage on the terrified accountant.

"Someone is disrupting our funds, our cash flow pipelines, everything! Millions gone without a trace!" The accountant shrank back, mumbling about cyberattacks and government surveillance.

"I suggest you find out where my money is. Get Marcus and his tech guys to track it down immediately—you have 24 hours!" he said, struggling to contain his anger.

The accountant's face turned white as he nodded profusely and made a swift exit. Prince appeared unhinged as paranoia seeped into the cracks, further compounding the problem.

He turned towards the camera as if sensing he was being watched. Leaning in for a closer view, he flipped the audio switch.

***

Buried deep at the back of the compound, a makeshift social club cluttered with alcohol and smuggled goods, served as an informal gathering point for Prince's men to speak freely. The scent of expensive cigars barely masked the underlying tension. Vincent broke the silence.

"Damn feds. Sticking their nose in our shit. This could get ugly."

Andrew exhaled a cloud of smoke. "Why now? Where's all this extra attention coming from?"

"No idea, but Prince has to do something," said Vincent.

Francis Matayer, a wiry-looking man in his 40s with a deep scar running across his face chimed in. "Who's got the fucking nerve to move against us?"

Vincent shook his head. "Damien was right. We're spreading ourselves too thin—all this talk of global expansion."

"That fucking Lila," said Andrew, visibly irritated.

Vincent shrugged. "I like the broad—she's an earner. And smart too. But I heard about the move she pulled the other day in the meeting—some fucking balls, I tell ya. And Prince bought it."

"Yeah, Damien was pissed," replied Andrew.

Francis cocked an eyebrow. "You think the big guy's fucking her?"

Vincent let out a sigh. "No idea, but she's a piece of ass, even with all that crazy ink..." he said, his voice tapering off.

Benny leaned in, his tone low and suspicious. "Something's up with that broad, I swear."

"What do you mean?", asked Vincent, head tilted.

"You know Marcus? Our tech guy?" asked Benny.

"Of course. What about him?" Vincent replied.

"So, he had all these micro cameras installed, even in Prince's private elevator. One day, she gets in the lift. You know how she is—with those eyes, and the walk…"

Vincent leaned in, intrigued. "Yeah, and?"

"She heads up to Prince's office. About half an hour later, she's on her way down again. I'm watching her on the feed and—"

"Is this guy writing a novel? Spit it out, Benny!" Francis chimed in, waving his cigar in the air.

Chuckles erupted among the men.

"Alright, laugh it up. But listen, she goes ballistic in there—arms flailing, smacking her own head, like she's fucking ubatz."

"Really? Was that before, or after you tried to fuck her?" Vincent said, nudging Benny's huge muscular frame.

The room dissolved into uncontrollable laughter once more.

"Yeah, yeah. Anyway, Elevator stops, and she pops out like nothing happened—gives me a 'Hi Benny' with that icy stare, you know…"

"No shit?" Vincent remarked.

"I'm telling you, that broad's got a few bodies in her closet."

The men grew curious. Francis smirked. "Sounds like my ex-wife."

They erupted in laughter again, if only to briefly escape the unspoken anxieties in the air.

Vincent took a sip of his drink and set it down, his expression sobering. "Jokes aside, if Prince is getting influenced by this broad, it could be bad news for all of us."

"Well, pussy can do that," said Francis.

"Easy guys, the walls have ears," warned Andrew, making a sweeping motion across the room.

Prince took stock of the scene: Vincent questioning his leadership, and the unsettled energy of his men. He assessed their concerns not as a leader worried about his crew, but as a predator sizing up potential dissent within his pack.

If there was one thing he could not stand, it was the implication that his reign was not all-powerful. The very existence of doubt was a threat to his rule. To allow it to fester would not only compromise him, but everything he had built.

Prince rose to his feet with a sense of muted urgency. He navigated his way to the makeshift council chamber where they were all held up. Each step he took was calculated and purposeful. He approached, walking right into the midst of their gathering, a wolf among sheep.

The blade moved almost faster than sight, grazing Vincent's neck with a surgical flick. Time stood still for a heartbeat as if waiting for grim reality to catch up. His eyes widened in slow realization, then the gush. Blood poured, turning his crisp white shirt crimson as he collapsed, his hands scrambling in vain. Vincent's expression was a deathly mix of surprise and anguish as the room froze. Gasps filled the space, followed by silence.

He lay struggling to breathe, his mouth opening and closing in futile attempts as life drained.

Prince wiped the blood-stained knife on Francis' sleeve, leaving it to seep into the fabric.

"What's the fucking joke?" Prince asked, closing in.

"Huh? What?" Francis blinked, off-kilter.

"You and your pals—giggling like a bunch of schoolgirls—must have been a hell of a joke," Prince insisted.

Francis stuttered, "Ah, we were just—"

The sentence died in his throat as Prince's fist slammed into his gut. Francis folded—in a fit of choking and coughing.

"Get up. We're at fucking war. Act like it," Prince shouted at the top of his lungs. "Unless you want to be digging a hole for yourself alongside Vincent."

Francis staggered upright, his hands spread in a futile gesture to quell Prince's fury. "I'm sorry, boss. I'm sorry."

Prince scanned their faces. "That's quite alright Francis. I can appreciate how some of you may be feeling 'unsettled' by Vincent's untimely demise, but I want you to know that my door is always open."

The room fell silent, none daring to engage or even make eye contact.

"Andrew," Prince's tone turned chillingly polite, "when you see Damien, tell him I want him in my office. Immediately."

"Yes boss, no problem boss," he replied.

With his point made, Prince left the men to dispose of Vincent's body.

A sour taste crept into my mouth as I assessed the full extent of Rhea's interference—it had to be her. She had played me with false hope and misdirection - dangling the possibility of ensnaring Prince in my trap, only to sink the entire plan at the most opportune moment.

For months, I had planned and orchestrated every move to bring down this organization. Every player was in place, every contingency accounted for. But now, standing amid a charged atmosphere, my strategy was unraveling. Not by my own mistake, but by a hidden saboteur.

The realization was bitter; Rhea, my elusive alter ego, clearly excelled at this game. And I could sense she was going in for the kill, but where she would strike next remained a mystery.

Either way, I couldn't afford to give up. I had sacrificed too much already. I had to salvage the situation no matter the cost.

Act III

The Dispensation of Rhea

Chapter 22
Ravaged Pt. 1

I moved under a sky devoid of stars, like a creature in heat; stalking the corridors of Prince's compound with cold-blooded intent. The chaos I had sown now bore fruit, disrupting his operations on multiple levels. His temper was flaring, paranoia creeping in. Now was the time to strike.

Approaching the heavy oak door to his private study, I steadied my breath. This was delicate, requiring finesse. I would fan the flames and present myself as a balm amidst the tumult.

I turned the brass handle as the door swung open without a sound. Solemn darkness enveloped the study, its walls sheathed in red velvet that swallowed the scant light. Black leather furniture held court, surrounded by the aromatic haze of cigar smoke and accompanied by shelves brimming with vintage spirits in elegant decanters.

Excellent. He was vulnerable, lost in the depths of a bottle. My approach was slow and deliberate, each step an alluring sway of my hips. I removed my fur coat and draped it over the armchair before perching myself on the edge of his desk. I slid my dark locks to one side, letting the warm light accentuate my features while he glanced up, eyes clouded.

"You need to see this," I said, handing him a folder carefully laced with my scent.

"What's this?" he slurred.

"It's the reason the feds are moving against us."

"What?" he jerked, alcohol diminishing his composure.

"We've been putting the screws to one of their major assets who fears exposure. He's refusing to cooperate, and they're pissed."

"Who?"

"Anderson Cavello—money mover to the rich, degenerate scumbag. They want his client list, bad."

"Maggot! I ought to blow up his life immediately."

"It's not my place to say, but I think rash decisions might be fueling the situation."

"You're right, it's not your place," he said, waving his glass as the fine whisky swished over the rim and seeped into the wooden floor.

"I'm just saying—the men seem rattled, and morale is low. Vincent's 'departure' probably didn't help either."

"Who the fuck do you think you are?" he fired off, lazily tilting back his head.

"I'm the only one here providing answers. And forgive me for speaking out of turn, but with the type of deal I'm working on, none of these cowards would dare turn their backs."

"Look at you, with your sultry eyes and sexy outfit. Behind that cold exterior and all those tattoos, you're nothing but a temptress," he said.

"I use what I have to survive, no different from you. And we both know I'm much more than a temptress."

"So you admit it!" Prince said with an intoxicated smirk, extending his hand toward my toned legs, accentuated by acutely pointed heels.

"I'm here talking business, and you're thinking about my ass? You've had too much to drink. You need to slow down," I said as I eased his hand away and repositioned myself further out of reach.

"Don't tell me what I need. Come here," he growled in frustration.

He lunged with one hand gripping my throat, and the other sliding between my thighs. My head snapped back in feigned protest, but my dark red lips and gritted teeth suggested otherwise.

And with that, he was no longer the cold, calculated criminal mastermind. He was merely a man with primal urges, unwittingly seduced by a woman who was the architect of his demise.

In a lustful rage, he pinned me down, removed my silk and lace underwear, and forcefully entered me. I put up a mild struggle for show, but he was already possessed. He groped and pounded, boring deep inside, with my body wedged awkwardly between his frame and the rattling desk.

Now, with Lila's vessel to command his pleasure, I allowed him to ravage me with complete disregard.

"Prince, STOP," I demanded.

"You've been begging for this the moment you walked into my office," he asserted.

"Prince, you're drunk. Stop," I persisted, knowing this would only encourage him.

"Shut the fuck up," he said. Before I had a chance to fully comprehend the words, I felt a harsh sting that resounded in my ears.

A second slap confirmed he was striking my face. It was an odd sensation as my tattoos seemed to writhe and react in defense.

But there was no resistance on my part. My body was almost limp as he flipped me over to face him.

I groaned as he peeled my legs back towards my chest with both hands gripping my ankles.

It felt as if he was trying to snap my limbs out of the sockets. The pain was exquisite.

"You want to be a part of my world? Fine," he said, as he bore down on me, unseating the motley array of objects on the desk. He was relentless as papers and stationary scattered and hit the floor.

"Does this make you feel like a man?" I gasped, as my words and body jerked in sync with his penetration.

His hand clamped around my throat, hoisting me upright with a violent tug. "You got something to say?" he barked. I stumbled, thrown off balance by a heel discarded.

"I'm going to break you," he proclaimed.

"Fuck off," I fired back, my words goading him.

"I admire your spirit, Lila."

He gripped tighter still, setting my neck muscles ablaze as he squeezed and choked off my air. Blood rushed to my head, causing my ears to pop. The fog of unconsciousness began to unfurl.

"No, no, no—I'm not done with you." He punctuated each word with a quick succession of light slaps to my face.

I laughed, staring him down as my faculties returned. "Is that it?" I taunted. His face twisted in a snarl.

I inhaled, arms dropping to my sides, completely open to whatever he could unleash.

I was stripped naked and dragged by my hair over to the couch. Then thrown head first, landing on all fours, dazed and disorientated.

The acute pain returned as he entered me again from behind, this time more aggressive, more forceful. He ploughed deeper and deeper, as if trying to extract a submission. As my body recoiled violently from the thrusts, I watched him—a man believed to be so powerful, and calculated, reduced to nothing more than a base creature.

He approached climax, tugging at my hair wrapped around his hand. With my back arched at a near-impossible angle, he continued to thrust as the pace quickened. I felt my inner walls stretch as he finally quaked, filling me with his life essence.

He caved, folding over me in exhaustion, emitting an animalistic growl.

"You're some broad!" he said, heaving, trying to catch his breath.

"You have no idea. Now get the fuck off me."

He pulled out, attempting to regain a semblance of composure.

I lay discarded, my knees bruised, legs buckled, with Prince's residue running down my thighs.

He fell back into his chair, body slouched, arms draped over the side.

His customary tailored hair was now disheveled, with his face marred by sweat.

At that precise moment, I couldn't tell you which I relished more—the thought of tormenting Lila with vivid flashbacks, or feasting on the sexual energy I cultivated. As for Prince—he was a prop I could have disposed of in a heartbeat. But he was right. I was aroused, lustful even, but not for him—for me. The pain sharpened my senses, revealing an ability to siphon the vigor of men for my own sustenance.

I pushed myself off the couch, each movement a deliberate act of defiance. I noticed my heels, strewn haphazardly near the desk, cast off in a moment of struggle. I approached and leaned against the sturdy frame. Gathering the first shoe, I slid my foot inside, planting it firmly on the floor. Reaching for the second, I repeated the process, completing the transformation from supposed prey to predator.

Once upright, my shoulders squared off, dispelling any trace of weakness. I stood naked, yet adorned with hidden knowledge spiraling around my body like a living scroll. There was no slump of defeat, no arch of submission.

"We're alike, you and me," Prince noted, studying the woman before him through a lens of fascination and contempt.

"Really? How so?" I enquired, indulging his delusions.

"We both understand—the only thing that matters in this world is power."

"True," I acknowledged. "But we're nothing alike."

"Is that right?" he replied.

"Yes. You regard power as force exerted. But genuine power is the silent whisper that warps the minds of kings and minions alike, bringing all to heel."

"What?" he questioned, confused.

I strode toward his ensuite bathroom. I wanted him to see—to know that despite the marks he had left, I could be neither tamed, nor broken.

My heels echoed against the opulent marble floor. The fluorescent light above cast an unforgiving glow on my battered form. Yet, intense gratification permeated my veins. I longed for the moment Lila would awake in the aftermath of the nauseating spectacle. The marks would serve as a reminder, not of Prince's domination of this body, but rather my domination over Lila's entire being. She would be confronted with the violation of her sanctity, her very identity commandeered for my dark amusement.

I slid on the silk and lace thong that she would find smeared with traces of the ordeal. The tight-fitting black dress, now torn, came next, followed by my fur coat that swirled around me like a dark spirit. I intentionally bore his sweat, the marks, and the bruises—each a remnant of this fateful night.

Drawing in a deep breath, I was enveloped by the aroma of Prince's cologne that lingered on me. I returned to the study where he sat, now clad in a smoking jacket, nursing a glass of aged scotch.

He looked up, his face a well-practiced mask of indifference. "Leaving so soon?"

"I'm afraid so," I replied, clasping my purse.

"Perhaps you got what you came for," he said, exhaling a thick cloud of smoke.

I held fast as the fog dissipated, salivating over the moment I would extinguish his life. He, in turn, remained blinded, grappling with inconsequential misdirection.

Unbeknownst to Prince, the axis of power had already tilted, nudging the scales beyond his purview. With a sharp turn, I head toward the door, pausing only to glance over my shoulder. "Good night, Mr. Prince."

As the door closed behind me, my next move was already in play—one that would send huge shockwaves through his beleaguered organization. The path to victory was set, and no force could deter me. The night was mine, and the world would soon follow.

Chapter 22
Ravaged Part 2

I awoke in the middle of my living room, face down, to a searing pain tearing through my nerves. Stumbling to my feet, my legs gave way, while my insides screamed in revolt.

Clutching the doorpost, I drew a shaky breath. Off-kilter and disoriented, the pain split my insides with every attempt to move.

As lucidness found me, the truth emerged from the rubble in all its violating enormity. Rhea had seized the reins, commandeering my body while my consciousness remained locked away, powerless to stop the depravity inflicted upon it.

Memories of each dehumanizing act ignited waves of nausea. Every inch of skin felt foreign and tainted. Her twisted psyche had overwritten my will, to sate desires I recoiled from. She rendered me a lifeless doll, discarded when the abuse was over. A potent cocktail of anger, shame, and visceral disgust swallowed me. I never imagined myself so disempowered—reduced to mere flesh and bone for the whims of my own fractured mind.

I caught a glimpse of my reflection in the mirror—hair disheveled, clothes torn and stretched. The woman staring back at me through smeared makeup was a soulless husk of a shell.

My fingers traced the contusions marking my neck, breasts, stomach, thighs—dark fingerprints of cruelty. The bloom of purple and blue was not just skin deep, it pierced my very being. Ghostly warmth and unwanted penetration still lingered, entwined with the ache of injuries sustained.

I found no respite as I attempted to scrub away the stench of stale sweat and sex. Clenching the porcelain sink, I hung onto the last vestiges of a self I recognized. Each thud of my heartbeat amplified the emptiness that spread from my chest to the tips of my fingers.

It was hard to breathe, harder still to think. The urge to yield to the crushing weight—to let myself be swept away into oblivion loomed large. On the edge, I wavered, tempted to surrender entirely and become an empty vessel once and for all.

And then, as if some inner threshold had been crossed, the dam broke. A guttural cry erupted from the bowels of my being, tearing through the silence and shredding my eardrums. It was a primal sound, unfiltered—more akin to the howl of a wounded animal than any human expression. My voice ricocheted off the tiles, filling the confined space and penetrating every crevice.

A second cry followed, then a third, each distinct yet woven together by raw emotion, forming an auditory hellscape of my own making. I felt my vocal cords strain, nearly reaching the point of rupture. The screams kept coming, each more wrenching than the last, as though my very soul were being exorcised.

There I was, broken, consumed by shame, disgust, and a deep-rooted sense of failure I couldn't shake. The impulse was too strong to resist. My fist made contact with the mirror surface, splintering it upon impact. Fragments cascaded down, crashing against the bathroom sink. My reflection shattered along with it.

With trembling fingers, I grabbed one of the pointed remnants and raised it to my face. The sharp, jagged edge glinted momentarily under the bathroom light before sinking into my skin. The cut was deep, slow, and deliberate, a grim reckoning slicing through black ink and white flesh. Blood oozed, thick, dark, and hot, running down my cheek.

The scattered pieces refracted my image, broken and distraught. What burned further still was the glimmer of satisfaction peering back at me. She was there, watching, relishing each moment. A parasitic twin, feasting on not just my body but my misery. There was an unsettling, almost carnal gratification she gained from this, one that transcended any form of conventional pleasure.

The thought anchored me, a loathsome realization that clung to my conscience. What kind of sick, twisted joy could be derived from the desecration of one's own host?

We were two entities locked in a perverse symbiosis, bound by blood and flesh, yet at constant war with each other. In her perverse reality, my demise was her ascent, my disarray, her equilibrium. In the unforgiving landscape of my own consciousness, she mapped my demise with the skill of a seasoned tactician. Her sadistic laughter served as the score to my unraveling. She had proven to be more cunning, more ruthless, and more capable. Even Prince, as he eviscerated my very being, fed her insatiable spirit.

Yet, as I longed for the serene nothingness that lay beyond, a peculiar sensation pricked at the edge of my despair, like thousands of insects scuttling over parched ground.

My tattoos pulsed, and a migraine loomed as if fighting to take hold. Yet this internal fire contrasted with an external chill. Fumbling through the shattered pieces around me, I searched for my own reflection.

What met my gaze defied belief: the gash on my cheek wavered. The tingling amplified, as though my tattoos were rallying to counter a hostile force. My skin began an intricate process of self-restoration, as molecules interwove and merged. I observed, captivated and bewildered, as my appearance reverted to its unmutilated form.

I probed and stretched the recently healed skin, half-expecting it to reopen at the lightest touch. All that remained was bruised flesh, a lingering reminder of the pain inflicted.

Stunned and confused, my altered mind flooded with an onslaught of questions. How was this even possible? Was my rapid healing due solely to the serum, or could it be a trait embedded in my genetic fabric? Had Dr. Shore chosen me for a reason beyond mere chance? Her timely appearance at my bedside seemed to suggest as much. Then there was Rhea—why hadn't she intervened to prevent me from mutilating the vessel she sought to command? Was she aware of my rapid self-healing? What other latent abilities existed within me, poised for emergence?

At that critical juncture, an epiphany occurred. It wasn't mere contempt that drove her; it was intense, caustic envy. She lusted after what was intrinsically mine, hankered for it to such an extent that she would resort to the vilest means to make me abdicate—to distort my perception until I viewed my own essence as a scourge. She aimed to make me detest my very being—allowing her to seize my body like the true parasite she is.

Just then, I heard Sam's voice. The memories hit me like a cool summer breeze, dislodging the mental fog that shrouded my thoughts. I found myself back in that remote stretch of California woodland, her laughter pulling me from the void of despair.

"...sure, get us lost in the middle of nowhere," I said, as I popped the hood of the car.

The old SUV had coughed its last on a desolate road, miles from any sign of civilization.

"We're not lost; we're on an unscheduled adventure," Sam replied, leaning against the car in her shorts, crop-top and hiking boots.

"Is that what you call this? You should've been an attorney, babe."

"I'll stick to journalism—where the truth actually matters!" She smiled, checking her phone for a signal.

"Well, then, Ms. Journalist, any ingenious ideas?"

"Actually, yes," Sam said, her eyes lighting up. "Remember that episode of 'MacGyver'? The one where he fixes a car engine using nothing but a paperclip, chewing gum, and a pocket knife?"

"I do, but we're neither MacGyver nor do we have a paperclip or chewing gum."

"Ah, but we have something better. Duct tape and zip ties!" Sam pulled the items from the trunk like a magician revealing a final trick.

"You're kidding. This isn't one of your exposés; we can't just duct tape our way out of this."

"Watch me." And she actually did it. With a blend of journalistic curiosity and reckless optimism, Sam had patched up the radiator long enough to limp the car to a service station. We laughed until we couldn't breathe—the absurdity of it all.

"How did you..." I began, still catching my breath between giggles.

"Trade secret, darling," she winked.

"I always said, 'Samantha Webb, that woman's going places,' probably jail, but places nonetheless."

She laughed, tossing the duct tape back into the trunk. "Well, let's just say I prefer the road less traveled."

I shook my head, grinning. "You sure do babe. You sure do!"

I returned to the wreckage of the bathroom as the memory faded into the distance. Suddenly, it all came in to focus—my current dilemma was yet another untrodden path that required me to stay the course, and crawl to the finish line if I had to. How could I allow myself to wallow in despair, when Sam had fought her own battles with a lion's courage? Her fearless attitude, her very constitution, became my guiding star for navigating the treacherous road ahead.

I looked again at the unbroken surface of my skin, an undeniable testament to my ability to overcome. I was Cora, yes, an amalgam of human frailties and imperfections. But coiled within was Lila, a resilience shaped by unimaginable adversity, a warrior, a survivor. Two sides of an equation, contrasting but essential aspects of a whole. And in this perilous world, I could ill afford to be just one or the other.

A stricken soul I may be, yet in anguish, I found clarity. I would emerge radiating a strength that could never be diminished. Somehow, I would find a way to salvage my mission and end Prince's reign. As for Rhea, with all her sadistic proclivities, she was nothing more than a parasite, feeding off my vulnerability. She underestimated me, for there was no extremity I wouldn't endure, no chasm I wouldn't cross to purge her from existence. And in due course, she would come to grasp that the creature she'd awakened was not forged from sinew and bone, but from a logic far more ominous, bent solely on scripting her demise. And it was there, in that underestimation, that I glimpsed my opening.

She wanted to exploit the scars she'd inflicted. But with each deception, I would deploy my own countermeasure. With every piece of me that she thought she claimed, I would take something of hers—an eye for an eye.

I felt this realization solidify, converting my vulnerability into something more robust—a resilient core, enveloped in quiet but steely determination. I traced back through past confrontations, analyzing each failure and setback. Rhea exploited my emotions, using pain and trauma against me.

However, the brain was just neurons firing, neurotransmitters fluctuating. If biological processes could be controlled, so could Rhea's mental sabotage. Her arsenal was cruelty and manipulation. I would counter with knowledge and discipline. She would whisper horrors to shatter my defenses—I would build psychological armor to weather her assaults. Where she sought to fragment me, I would integrate using sheer willpower. And I would hide some part of myself, an impenetrable fortress locked away from her corruption.

In this uncharted battle of wills, I'd remained steadfast, choosing to bide my time and wait for the ideal opportunity to strike. I would use her to achieve my goals—and on that day, I'd rise unbroken from the ruins she had made of my life.

Chapter 23
In His Wake

Prince's stronghold buzzed with urgency as I arrived two days later—still feeling sick to my stomach at the thought of past events. Guards patrolled the perimeter with heightened alertness and guns at the ready. Blacked-out SUVs left tire marks as they sped away, ladened with men clad in military fatigue. Radio static broke through the morning's silence with bursts of coded conversation. It seemed I had come dressed for the occasion; donning snug leather pants, a bomber jacket, knee-high boots, and eyes shielded by dark glasses.

Staff hurried along corridors with their heads buried as I strode into the security room. We had a full house, all the guys were there, busy and frantic. Multiple screens flickered with real-time data, maps, and surveillance footage. Phones rattled sporadically on the wooden table in the center of the room that bore the weight of multiple stacks of documents, hard drives, and disposable coffee cups.

Marcus was engrossed in a phone conversation, hastily jotting down notes. He flashed a warm smile as he glanced in my direction. Francis shuffled through a stack of papers, carefully scanning lines of transactions. Meanwhile, Vic, a sturdy man with a pockmarked face, stood attentively in front of multiple surveillance monitors. In the background, several individuals were diligently hunched over laptops, with earpieces securely in place.

Marcus spun around to face me as he hung up. "You look rough babe. Run into trouble?" he said, noticing my discolored face behind the glasses.

"Something like that. What's going on?"

He examined me for a beat longer. "Damien's missing. Prince is pissed."

"Missing? How? When?" The urgency in my voice betrayed more concern than I'd wanted to show.

"Two... actually three days now. No one's seen anything. CCTV is blank," Marcus said.

"For fuck sake! What has she done now?" I thought to myself.

I looked over at Vic, who was still absorbed in the screens. "You find anything?" I asked him.

"Zilch. Like he vanished into thin air," he replied.

Raising an eyebrow, I asked Marcus, "And how's Prince taking it?"

He winced, his voice dropping to a hushed tone. "Like a cat trapped in the corner, with its tail on fire."

My pain was momentarily eclipsed by a muffled laugh. Humor was always welcome, especially at Prince's expense. "That bad, huh?"

"He's making life hell for everyone around him. You don't want to be the messenger of bad news today," Marcus added.

He continued, "He's ready to burn bridges to find Damien, literally."

"How so?" I enquired.

Marcus looked around, ensuring that we weren't overheard. "Let's just say he's got some guys who aren't exactly known for their diplomacy—the kind that shoots first and then blows shit up after."

"I see. Bringing out the big guns, then," I remarked.

"Yes, but it's a risky move. You have to be careful who you're aiming at," Marcus said, exhaling a deep breath.

"He's been making a few rash decisions lately," I added.

"You sure you ok? Those are some nasty bruises—I hope you carry a gun. You know we have an armory, right?"

"I've been meaning to check it out—thanks, Marcus,"

"I can give you a few lessons if you like?" he offered.

"…I picked up a thing or two from my best friend. She's from Arizona—learning to shoot was almost a rite of passage—I never liked guns though," I admitted.

"Hell, use a cattle prod if you have to! You need something."

"You're right. Thanks Marcus," I said with a friendly jab to the shoulder.

He smiled and continued. "Anyway, Prince is scrubbing through everyone in the inner circle—re-evaluating. It's like a witch hunt."

I felt a twinge of concern, quickly suppressed. "That means we're all under the microscope."

"Everyone and everything," he confirmed. "So, if you've got any skeletons, now's the time to bury them deeper."

"Sounds like you have a few secrets of your own, Marcus."

"Yea, well, this is not exactly the career I had in mind, Lila," he said, his tone belying a sense of solemn regret.

His words had barely settled when the door burst open with such force it rebounded off the wall. Everyone in the room looked up with an immediate halt in their movements.

Prince stormed, his face taut with restrained fury. Two heavily armed goons followed him in, scanning the room as if expecting to find an enemy lurking in the corners.

"Wait outside," Prince barked at them. They hesitated for a split second before retreating, closing the door behind them.

Every eye in the room was on Prince, mine most of all, as I turned to face him. Despite all that I had been through, I had never contemplated taking a life until that very moment. I knew without question it was something I was capable of, and I felt oddly at peace with this harrowing recognition.

Marcus observed the subtle stand-off, his attention shifting from Prince to me and back again. He kept his head down, knowing better than to trip over someone else's steps.

"What have we got?" Prince shot in his direction.

Marcus jumped to it, outlining the development. "Three safe houses turned inside out. Nobody's talking."

"Then make them scream," Prince replied.

"Yes sir," Marcus said.

A buzz cut through the air as a burner phone vibrated on the table. "Ivan" flashed on the screen. Prince snatched it up. "Well?"

"We're at the warehouse. These guys are bleeding out. If they knew anything, they'd have spilled it by now."

"Get rid of them. Don't call back until you have something."

Ivan's muffled "You got it, Boss," was barely audible before Prince ended the call with a jab of his thumb.

His glare swept the room. "Listen up, all of you. Damien is your number one priority. Find him!"

"And where's Andrew, that fat fuck? I want him here now," Prince demanded.

"We'll try to get hold of him, sir," Marcus replied.

"Boss, we got a lead on the stolen funds from your account. Could be connected," said Francis, waving a handful of files.

Prince's nostrils flared. "Then follow it. Track the account. See where it leads."

Had Rhea dropped me in it? Were my fingerprints on the paper trail? I had to remain calm and let things play out.

"Lila, a word," Prince said, gesturing for me to join him out of earshot of the others.

I pivoted, considering him for a moment before nodding curtly. We moved toward a corner of the room.

"...about the other night..." he pre-empted, noticing the dark bruises now adorning my neck like a collar of shame.

"It's unimportant, I prefer to focus on more pressing matters," I interrupted, although now the thought of being anywhere near him made me sick to my stomach.

"That's what I like about you, Lila. You see the big picture."

"Sure," I replied, as my emotions flared, exacerbated by the dull ache in my body every time I shifted weight.

Vic's voice interrupted. "Boss, got something. Damien's phone pinged near the docks a few days ago, around 1 p.m. Then it went dark."

Prince's gaze cut to Vic. "Get a team there. Now."

"Fuck, this can't be good. I need to get out of here," I thought to myself.

"Maybe I should go. Keep an eye on things from a distance and report back," I interjected.

Prince sized me up with skepticism. "Since when did you care so much about Damien? You two were never exactly buddies."

"I don't need to like someone to appreciate their utility. You, of all people, should know that, Prince."

"Utility can be fickle, Lila. One minute you're indispensable; the next, you're a placeholder. Now loyalty, that's a rare trait. Something Damien understands. Odd that his sudden absence seems fortuitous for some."

"Nature's unpredictability—it's hard to know the root cause sometimes," I replied.

Prince studied me and shot back. "Some roots are better cut than left to rot."

"A useful notion. But if not careful, one could end up chopping down the whole damn tree." I said bluntly.

Prince remained silent, contemplating my barbed insubordination on full display.

The entire room had witnessed my veiled challenge to his authority. As callous as he was, Prince couldn't dismiss his startling fall from grace only a few nights ago. For a man who had cultivated a veneer of strength and self-control, he had sullied his own ego, allowing a "mere woman" to reduce him to nothing more than a base creature, like so many of the pathetic targets we exploited.

Yet, I sensed further weakness. Damien was a key member of the organization, sure, but Prince didn't strike me as one for sentimentality. Why was Damien's disappearance now the main priority? Even above business?

Was Prince concerned with his organization appearing vulnerable? Or was this a more personal matter?

"Marcus, did you speak to our guy at the FBI about Anderson Cavello? It's Lila's intel, so I expect it to be…reliable," Prince said, never once looking away from me.

"Not yet, I'm still trying, boss," he said, sounding dubious.

"Shit, who the hell was Anderson Cavello?" I asked myself. This wasn't good. I needed to get out of here.

"Prince, there are matters concerning our international expansion that require immediate attention. If you need me, I'll be on my cell," I informed him.

"Is this how you abandon ship? At a time like this?" he asked.

"Hardly. I've invested too much in this deal to leave it languishing. Besides, international waters could provide a much-needed boost to our power base—as we discussed the other night, remember?" I remarked, my tone laced with ice.

"Fine, do what you have to. But get back here immediately afterward," he conceded.

Prince's fixation on finding Damien had made the atmosphere even more volatile. Was it a meticulous distraction Rhea had engineered, or a happy accident she was sure to exploit?

My only option hinged on compiling the evidence I'd gathered on his illicit dealings and funneling it to Mack; he was perhaps the one person willing to act.

Vic interrupted my thoughts. "Boss, we found Damien's car near one of our warehouses off Highway 299—keys still in the ignition. Our guys are on their way."

His words almost stopped me dead in my tracks as I exited the room, weaving past the guards still stationed outside.

If Damien turned up dead, I would be the prime target of Prince's suspicions, and his quest for vengeance that would no doubt follow. I hastened through the corridor, feet barely touching the ground, eager to distance myself from the impending crisis. Just as the exit came into view, a voice thundered my name from the rear.

"Ms. Thompson."

"Shit," I thought, picking up the pace.

The voice got louder. "Ms. Thompson, hold on!" they shouted.

"I've got to go," I said, not slowing.

I reached the security box and attempted to dart past it.

"Lila, wait up," said Max, the head security guard, fiddling with his radio.

"I really need to go," I insisted.

"Just one moment," he replied.

This wasn't good. There was a trio of armed guards stationed like gargoyles at the gate, sharpshooters above, and Prince's own guard dogs sniffing at my heels. I was cornered. My hand twitched towards my hairpin when Marcus burst onto the scene.

"Lila, you forgot these," he gasped, handing me my sunglasses.

I masked my confusion as I played along in full view of the guards watching. "Oh yeah, your hunch about Cavello? Looks like you were right… reliable as always!" he said, his casual words masking his solemn expression.

I knew something was off. Cavello was Rhea's intel, not mine. Whatever she told Prince would most likely crumble under scrutiny. Marcus must have already known, and he was warning me.

"No problem. I'll catch you later," I said, flicking my shades and turning to leave.

The gates opened slowly, and then slammed shut, sealing off the world behind me as I made my hasty exit and disappeared out of sight. Marcus had intervened just in time, yet the close call amplified the gravity of what lay ahead. This was a highly volatile situation, and it was just a matter of time before everything erupted.

Prince, Damien, Rhea—all variables in an equation that were growing increasingly complex. But one thing was clear: In this arena of power plays and veiled motives, I would either avenge Sam, or fall victim to the same fate, or worse—be engulfed by the demon that now festered within me.

Chapter 24
Rhea's Declaration

Damien. My rival. My irritation. My tool. Since our last encounter, the fastidious Mr. Black had taken it upon himself to pry into my affairs. Ever the diligent boyscout, he seemed to be highly proficient in piecing together truths about Dr. Shore and the mysterious serum that had freed me from my confinement. Despite hours of relentless torture, he refused to divulge how he had come to possess such insightful information—almost as if the Ring may have had prior dealings with her in some capacity.

In any case, this was a loose end I could not leave flapping in the wind. Damien had to be swiftly removed from the equation.

The vacancy had created a schism within the organization, a timely imbalance. Prince's obsession with uncovering the truth was not a threat, but a sign of emotional weakness. Little did he know that while he ravaged me, Damien's body was already cold—such was the irony.

I observed the ripples of my actions, noting Lila's growing resolve and inner strength, understanding that she was unknowingly moving according to my hand.

Each revelation, and each turn of the plot, was a new layer to be folded seamlessly into my design. Lila was on the verge, and I, hidden, was nudging her forward towards our shared fate.

As I surveyed the landscape of ordered chaos, I knew I held the reins. Complacency, however, was not in my nature.

To this end, I crafted something to illuminate Prince's path and provide Lila with the motivation to embrace her true essence. With a flourish, I wrote the words inked in Damien's own blood, each stroke a piece of the puzzle I had laid out for him. This letter would inflame him in ways mere words could never accomplish. It was more than a message; it was an invitation, a challenge, a declaration of war.

I savored each word as if they were the sweetest morsels of forbidden knowledge. All secrets laid bare, from Lila's concealed identity to my intentions, or rather, destiny, to ascend the throne and mold a divine rule in my image.

I sealed the envelope and allowed myself a moment of satisfaction. Prince would receive it, and follow where it led, like a moth to a flame. He would discover the truth behind Damien's end, and in the process, become further blinded by his own fury. Prince, like all who've stood in my way, would realize that his reign was but a prelude to something of far greater magnitude.

Chapter 25

Revelations

A sharp knock on the door severed Prince's train of thought. "Come," he commanded. It swung open, one of his men appeared, holding a letter.

"This came for you, boss. Via courier," he said, placing the sealed envelope on his desk.

"From who?" Prince inquired.

"Anonymous sender, boss. Security already scanned it. It's clean," the man replied.

"Close the door on your way out," Prince instructed.

The man promptly exited the office, as Prince turned his attention to the mysterious letter sitting on his desk. His fingers traced the wax seal briefly before breaking it. He unfolded the parchment and began to read.

"Prince, I'm sure you recognize the fragrance. An intimate detail meant just for you..." the letter opened with.

"What are you playing at Lila?" he wondered to himself.

The letter was a detailed account of treachery, the likes of which Prince would have lauded if he were not the victim. The mention of Samantha Webb, a name vague and foggy, almost eluded his memory. As he moved further down the page, he noticed the ink's unusual hue. Instinctively, he touched the writing, his finger coming away sticky.

"Top marks for theatrics," Prince said.

He read on, each line revealing a betrayal more audacious than the last. The fake charity set up as his personal honey trap. Then the assault on his digital fortress—his security protocols rendered useless by my infiltration. His eyes darted to the next revelation. Compromised bank accounts and liquidated assets—that earned a sneer.

The fiasco that led to the death of his men in the police ambush, and the vanishing act of Charlotte Garcia and fat Andrew—all meticulously orchestrated. And of course: his political allies defecting, swayed by the weight of confiscated leverage now in Rgea's possession.

She went on to reveal my scheme to implicate him in the international expansion deal. And the crowning blow: Damien's death only hours prior to Rhea's sultry appearance in his office. His finger paused.

"Fucking bitch," he exhaled, slowly shaking his head in disbelief.

Not to be upstaged, she delivered an encore. Enter my shadow self birthed from a volatile serum now poised to unseat him.

"Really? A fucking psycho?" Prince said in disbelief.

His grip tightened, crumpling the document as his patients wore thin.

"And it seems the good doctor had been busy. I should never have spared her," Prince remarked, alluding to their shared past.

"Call them in," he ordered, pushing the button for the speaker on his desk.

Minutes later, there was a knock at the door. In walked two muscular men clad in black army fatigues, their faces impassive. Outside, four additional men stood in military formation.

"Yes, sir?" said Sterling, the team leader, in an enquiring tone.

"Eliminate Lila. Annihilate Rhea," Prince ordered.

The men exchanged a brief glance. "Sir, are these two separate targets?" one of them finally asked, breaking the silence.

"It's the same crazy bitch. Just bring me her head," he corrected, his voice barely rising.

"Sir, do you mean...?" He paused, turning to his colleague for clarification.

"Would you like a demonstration?" Prince replied, glancing toward his cabinet of assorted weapons.

"No sir. Copy that sir," the man nodded.

"GPS coordinates will be sent to your device. Get moving," Prince ordered.

"Yes, sir," they replied in unison, exiting briskly.

"Sterling," Prince said, causing the men to stop in their tracks. "Something feels off here. Go in heavy," he warned.

"Copy that, sir," he replied as he glanced up, closing the door behind him.

The unmasking of this double-dealing was a personal attack on what Prince held most dear—his own sense of authority. The woman he had allowed into his organization was a harbinger of death, pushing him inexorably toward destruction.

***

Only a few miles on the other side of town, the atmosphere was muted, yet equally charged. I sat alone in my darkened apartment, fingers drumming the armrest of my chair. The space was now stark, shorn of all but the most essential furnishings. I contemplated the inevitable series of events that would follow. My senses were in overdrive: ears primed to catch the faintest sound, nose subtly detecting shifts in the air, and skin tingling in anticipation.

And as if providing a battle hymn for my impending doom, Rhea lurked, omnipresent.

"What?" I snapped, sensing her glee.

"So it seems you've finally come to appreciate my talents," she whispered in my ear.

"I can assure you, 'appreciate' isn't the word I'd use," I replied, uneasy about how comfortable I'd become in engaging with her voice.

"A cooperative hostage. How novel," she quipped.

"I have one goal. And I won't allow you or anyone else to stop me," I said.

A low laugh echoed in my mind. "Ah yes, justice, comfort for a fool."

"I've had enough of your philosophical diatribes," I replied, irritated.

"So, what's it going to be, Lila? The pretense of moral high ground is no longer a luxury you can afford."

Taking a deep breath, I spoke. "Don't think for a second this changes anything between us."

"How naïve," she scoffed.

"Maybe, but still better than being delusional," I retorted.

"Ah, pettiness. A clear sign you're embracing your darker instincts," she said.

"You got what you want. Now leave me in peace," I replied.

Deep down, I realized her actions were irreversible. She had backed me into a corner where ethics became abstract and nebulous. The odds of besting her were against me; she was a superior adversary. But I'd already made my countermove, leveling the playing field with a hidden failsafe should she prevail.

Then, at last, silence fell. The incessant chatter and grating moans dissipated; she was quiet. The world had muted, and I relished the fleeting tranquility, brief though it may be.

As I stood peering up at the midnight sky, I couldn't predict where this path would lead, but one thing was certain—while I promised to seek justice for Sam, I swore vengeance for myself.

Chapter 26
The Reckoning

I reached for Sam's old photograph on the shelf, brushing away the thin layer of dust that had settled over her face. There she was, wearing the pendant that still hung around my neck. My fingers closed around it, a tangible anchor, the same one I'd sought upon hearing of her passing.

Her smile radiated even though the picture had faded over time. I caught a glimpse of the carefree days we shared in what seemed like another lifetime. She awakened my courage and taught me how to fight for what I believed in. This confrontation was a simple, ruthless equation: retribution or death. And now, the moment had arrived to fulfill an unspoken pact, to pay tribute to both the girl she was and the martyr she had become.

I began prepping the arena, the likely ground zero of the imminent attack. Every vulnerability was transformed into a death trap for those foolish enough to enter. As I tightened a makeshift snare and calibrated the tripwires, every inch of my apartment became a killing field, and I intended to exploit that to the fullest extent.

As I peered through the side of my curtains, each shadow seemed deeper; every sound amplified. My senses, now fine-tuned to the slightest disruption, caught the anomaly. A distant, almost imperceptible sound ruptured the stillness of the night. Followed by a whisper of movement, a hint of danger. I took one last moment to center myself, every fiber of my being coiled in readiness.

And then, in an instant, a violent explosion detonated, obliterating the door and hurling splinters of wood and glass throughout the apartment.

A flashback resurfaced, but I was no longer the vulnerable prey they expected. I sidestepped the flying debris in a fluid motion and readied my blade to strike. The assassins, highly trained, moved with deadly precision, their expressions set in grim determination.

"Weapons hot. Go," a voice could be heard saying as shadows moved through the smoke.

As they advanced, traps triggered one by one. A sharp knife swung down from the ceiling, slicing through the air and embedding itself deep into the forehead of an assailant.

"Reno's down. Area is rigged. Repeat area is rigged."

A hairline cable was tripped by the foot of another intruder, instantly releasing a spray of barbed wire from the wall. His body tensed as the barbs dug in and tore at his flesh. He screamed until a swing of my blade ended his misery.

Another man shared a similar fate. A hidden snare looped around his ankle, hoisting him feet first in the air. Dangling, he fumbled for his weapon, but it was too late.

"Let me help you," I offered, before slashing upwards, cutting him across the abdomen. His screams pierced my eardrums until a second slash silenced him for good. A quick twist of the blade, and I severed the snare, sending him plummeting to the ground in a heap.

"Shit, Sterling down. Watch your six," I heard another intruder hiss through an earpiece.

My hands moved with a life of their own, guided by an instinct I had never known before. I struck hard—a brutal and unrelenting assault that left no room for mercy. Chaotic screams and clashes rang out as panic set in.

"What the...?" was all he managed before I opened him up and spilled his guts with a slash of my blade. Blood splattered on the walls, and bodies fell one by one. Arms and legs were severed, landing with a thud, separated from their owners who were now reduced to crawling, moaning heaps.

A man clutched the slit across his throat, gasping for air that would never come. Another, his eyes wide in disbelief, tried to stem the flow of life from his severed artery, but his hands, slick with blood, failed him. The atmosphere thickened with the stifled cries that marked their final moments. Each kill was a statement, a message of intent to Prince and his minions.

I surveyed the wreckage in the aftermath—the broken door, shattered glass, twisted metal, and mangled corpses scattered across the floor. The evidence was clear. I had crossed a line in my pursuit of justice, and there was no returning to the innocence I had lost. The waning rush only intensified my thirst for vengeance.

In a chilling declaration, I carved a single letter into each corpse's chest, arranging them in a gruesome message intended for Prince. I felt Rhea gyrate, her own morbid satisfaction beginning to seep into my subconscious, eroding the lines between her sadistic pleasure and my emerging blood lust.

***

Soon after, the news of the thwarted assassination attempt reached the organization. The reality differed vastly from Prince's anticipation.

"Team's wiped out, boss. Found them dumped at the gate," Max said, maintaining composure.

"Explain," Prince snapped.

"She read us like a book," Max continued. "Had the whole place rigged. I watched the live feed. She took them out single-handed." He shook his head.

"You're telling me Lila eliminated Sterling's whole team?" Prince replied in utter disbelief.

"They went in heavy like you said, boss. She took them apart. You had to see it," Max explained.

"We're talking about one woman—what the fuck!" Prince was dumbfounded. "Benny, find out if she's got muscle." The man promptly pulled out his phone and stepped away to make inquiries.

"Boss, have a look at this," Francis said, crouching beside the body bags.

"What am I looking at?" Prince peered at the dismembered corpses.

"There's writing on their chests," Francis replied, leaning in for a closer inspection.

"Spit it out, what's it say?" Prince snapped.

Francis hastened to solve the morbid puzzle. "M, Y, T, U..."

"MY TURN," Prince cut in, the words adding further insult to injury.

"Who the hell..?" Francis began, but let the question hang.

"You ever seen a broad like this? I'd trade ten of you for one of her," Prince quipped. "Get ready, she's coming—go!" he ordered, his voice laced with urgency.

"Who's coming?" Francis said, still trying to connect the dots.

"Fucking Lila. Who do you think? Moron," Prince shouted as the men sprang to their feet and darted towards defensive positions.

The realization dawned on him. I had metamorphosed into a formidable opponent, matching him move for move. With steely determination pumping through my veins, I prepared to wreak havoc on the man who thought himself untouchable.

Chapter 27
A Dark Path

Nightfall draped itself over the compound as pitch-black rain lashed the desolate grounds. With a Glock 45 pistol in one hand, samurai blade in the other, and a dagger strapped to my side—I stood ready for my final rendezvous with Prince.

Floodlights cut through the darkness as surveillance cameras swiveled, their mechanical lens searching for intruders. I approached, each step carefully measured—deadly, and silent, avoiding the attention of the armed guards patrolling the perimeter.

Breaching a hole in the fence created with cutters, I slid into a narrow recess, my back against the concrete wall. Glaring lights panned in my direction, followed by Max's gaze before he exchanged words with a guard, and disappeared inside. Narrowly missing exposure, I waited for the opportune moment when the man entered a blind spot. I struck as my hand muffled his gasp, and my blade found its mark in his side.

I took aim at the surveillance camera. One suppressed gunshot, and it was out of action. I crept further along the wall, spotting another guard preoccupied with shielding his lit cigarette from the rain. My blade whistled through the air before slicing across his chest. The force spun him around as he collapsed, enveloped by the dark.

Breaking into a sprint, I closed in on two more guards. Before they had a chance, my blade swiped from right to left, dropping the first, followed by a decisive thrust into the second. A burst of red mist escaped his mouth as I yanked the blade free. I unhooked his radio as his body slumped to the wet grass, life draining.

Keeping clear of the patrol, I kept low to the ground and advanced towards the main building.

The grand marble staircase loomed as radio chatter exploded. "Perimeter breached," a crackled voice declared over the radio. "Four casualties. I repeat, four casualties."

Max's voice seized the frequency. "It's her. Assume positions. Stay sharp."

Just then, the door at the top of the landing burst open. Reinforcements cascaded down, guns at the ready—each face familiar.

"Lila, stand down," Max shouted from behind cover.

"Gentlemen, I suggest you leave," I informed them. "My quarrel is with Prince, not you."

"That's not how this works, Lila. You know that," Max countered.

"Prince dies today. The only question is whether I splay you out alongside him."

"This bitch has lost it," said Francis.

Max shot him a stern look as he tried to de-escalate the situation. "Lila, this won't end well."

"Enough of this shit," Francis remarked before spraying automatic gunfire that peppered its way down the stairs.

"Fucking idiot," Max said under his breath.

"So be it." Without hesitation, my Glock roared back, sending bullets flying in their direction.

Blood sprayed the walls as multiple men fell from behind pillars and large decorative plants lining the balcony.

Benny and two other guards moved to flank me downstairs as they lunged from doors on either side. I pulled the trigger, hitting Benny twice in the chest, causing him to collapse as he slid down against the wall. Without missing a beat, I turned and let off four more rounds, launching the other two guards airborne. The force of the bullets sent them flying back, crashing through the doors from which they emerged.

A barrage of bullets hailed from above. I dodged, blade deflecting the few that came too close. I ascended further, using the sides for cover as I closed the distance. Each step was marred by blood and death, but my purpose remained clear.

Max maintained his post, guarding the corridor leading to Prince's private elevator. On the other side, Francis and two more men huddled. "What the fuck are you waiting for? Get her!" Francis barked, shoving them forward.

Seizing the moment of disarray, I acted without hesitation. I blasted one in the face and hurled my dagger at the other. They fell backward as blood splattered, lining the path as I reached the top of the staircase.

Francis made a desperate bid to escape, discharging his weapon over his shoulder as he scrambled for the door. I slipped the clip and reloaded, sinking five shots into his back as he screamed and buckled, falling over the balcony to his death.

I paused, surveying the fallen. Men lay heaped, life draining away. Only Max now stood in my path. Anchoring my foot on a guard's dead body, I dislodged the dagger and strode toward him.

"You can still leave Max," I said, blood dripping from the tip of the blade trailing my steps. "Is Prince really worth dying for?"

"No. But I don't run," he replied, resigned to his fate.

Without warning, he raised his gun and fired four shots in my direction. My sword came to life, deflecting each bullet. The subtle hum of steel filled the air as the smoke cleared, revealing that he'd been struck multiple times. He staggered back, clutching his neck leaking blood, before finally collapsing to the ground.

The distant creek of a door made me swivel abruptly, blade at the ready. "Lila, wait a second," Marcus called out from the corridor. He approached with his hands raised and his gun holstered.

He came closer, stepping over Francis and the other bodies piled on the floor.

"What the fuck? You did this?" he asked, stunned.

"I suggest you find a different line of work—very different," I emphasized.

He lowered his hands and stared at me.

"Cora Bishop!" he said.

I froze, momentarily losing composure.

"What did you say?" I asked through clenched teeth, hands tightening around my blade.

"Wo there!" he said, backing up nervously.

"I may not be a super hacker like yourself, but I'm no idiot. I figured out your connection to Samantha Web and Dr. Shore—I had nothing to do with either of them," he added promptly.

"What do you know?"

"…only that Prince had Damien working on a project not even I was privy to. Something personal, I suspect."

"You knew about Anderson Cavello, how?"

"I'd already done my homework. The man's no informant; he's an FBI agent through and through. Whoever gave you that intel has a wicked sense of humor."

"That's one way to put it," I replied. "Why did you help me, anyway?"

A shrug lifted his shoulders, and a faint smile traced his lips. "Call it professional courtesy."

"Is that so? In any case, I appreciate it," I told him. "…you should leave, Marcus."

"Are you hurt?" he asked, not ready to depart.

"I'm fine."

"I'm guessing you and Prince have unfinished business?"

"…soon to be concluded," pausing as my voice faltered. "He killed my only friend," the words slipped out as I lowered my sword.

He moved the blade aside tentatively and rested a hand on my shoulder. "I'm sorry, Cora," he uttered softly, now standing only inches away from my face. We exchanged a look, silently searching each other's eyes.

"Cora died a long time ago. Bye, Marcus." I withdrew, fighting to maintain the razor-sharp focus needed for what lay ahead.

"...Okay. Take care—Lila." He smiled briefly as his fingers slid away, the warmth of his touch soon to follow.

I watched him closely as he maneuvered past his fallen colleagues who now decorated the staircase.

As he reached the bottom, our gazes met one final time. "Lila," he said, his voice tender.

"Yes. Marcus," I replied, blunt and cold.

"Avoid the elevator. They're expecting you... and you may want to visit the armory before you head up there."

I remained silent, unable to voice my thoughts.

He gave a nod and vanished through a side door, erasing himself from my life's equation. And yet, there I was, on the verge of fulfilling my promise to Sam. Each dead body around me a symbol of the dark road I had embarked upon. A road paved with secrets, treachery, and unspoken horrors. My thoughts drifted for a moment—Marcus' words lingered. "Cora Bishop!" His utterance of that name was a stark reminder of a life I could no longer claim, a past I had forsaken in my quest for retribution.

For a heartbeat, I wondered what life could have been if not for this vendetta consuming me. My mind toyed with the fantasy—Sam laughing at one of my terrible jokes, a husband at my side whose biggest worry was the mortgage, and maybe, children. My own family, something wrenched away from me before I even understood its value.

My eyes betrayed me, moisture blurring my vision. I could feel the tension building in my skull. Despite the cold, calculated demeanor that had gotten me this far, my breaths now emerged shaky and almost erratic.

My stomach convulsed as if rejecting the cruel possibility of a life never lived. My grip tightened around the edge of the balcony, holding on to keep myself from spiraling into an emotional void.

"Really—Lila? Did you ever imagine there would be a white picket fence at the end of this road?"

And there she was, on cue, the bane of my existence. "Be—quiet, Rhea," I exhaled. "I don't need a pep-talk from you."

But she was right. Whatever the mental tug-of-war she initiated within me, it always concluded with ruthless clarity. My eyes dried up, emotion receding like a wave pulling back from the shore. I inhaled slowly, deeply, my grip easing off the rail.

My finger twitched back to life, finding comfort on the steel trigger. My blade, still stained with violence it had wrought, felt like an extension of me. Ahead lay the final door, behind which lurked the man responsible for Sam's death, and the dark deeds that had shattered countless children's lives.

My moment of reflection was over; what remained was the task at hand. I was ready. No more distractions, no more detours. I had defied the odds, and toppled Prince's main line of defense, and now it was time for our last encounter.

Chapter 28
A Beautiful Death

Elevator numbers climbed—2, 3, 4, 5—steadily ratcheting up the tension for the ill-fated encounter.

An arsenal of high-powered weapons targeted the steel doors. "She's on the move," a voice whispered.

6… "Hold," another voice ordered.

Clad in full tactical gear, Prince's elite guards watched as the numbers ground up with mechanical certainty.

7… "Ready…" Poised, with sweaty palms and twitchy fingers, they held the line, eager to shoot.

8… The elevator arrived with an understated ding.

Gunfire erupted as the doors parted, turning the lift's luxurious interior into a spectacle of ruptured glass and shredded wall panels.

"Stop!" shouted a man. "Where is she?" he asked, peeking around the side for a better view.

As the dust settled, a lone grenade pin dangled from the top of the door, oscillating like a pendulum of doom.

"Fuck. Pull back. Pull back…" they shouted, realization dawning too late.

A cataclysmic explosion devastated the lavish top floor, blowing out windows with smoke and shrapnel. Fire billowed, setting off sprinklers that collided with debris and embers.

Observing from a rooftop window, I broke cover, sliding through an air vent into the chaos below. My boots touched down amid the carnage, the smell of charred flesh all too familiar. Advancing towards Prince's office, I passed the grotesque aftermath of my ambush. Men lay scattered and dismembered across the floor, struggling to move. Their pleas for mercy were swallowed by the sound of gunshots as I executed them, one by one.

I stepped over chunks of statues, feared warriors once frozen in time, reduced to rubble almost indistinguishable from the men who lay beside them. As I reached the large ornate doors, an odd sense of calm washed over me. I could feel her dark, intoxicating influence absorbing my psyche—and I no longer resisted. My sole focus was Prince, held tightly in my grip, ready to suffer his inevitable fate.

As the door panned open, there he stood, trapped by the large window framing the city he once ruled with an iron fist. He raised an AR15 assault rifle and opened fire, but his bullets flew wide, squandering their lethal intent. Despite his dread, he persevered, firing again in defiance. I evaded the hail of bullets with lightning reflexes, seemingly in slow motion.

"Fuck!" Prince shouted in frustration. Out of ammo, he hurled his assault rifle at me.

Without missing a beat, I snatched it out of the air and discarded it nonchalantly.

"Is that it?" I asked, never once breaking my stride.

He charged, gripping a large combat knife with a glint of ill intent. I sidestepped, seizing his wrist and twisting until I heard the bone snap.

"Aghhh," he screamed, as his knife clattered to the floor.

"What's the matter? I thought you liked it rough?" I asked, savoring his pain.

A flurry of jabs to his midsection caused him to spit bile. He retaliated with strikes of his own, landing blows to my face, throwing me off balance.

"You know I'm never one to shy away from a bit of foreplay," he replied, winding up for another blow.

I exploited his split-second of hubris. A swift jab to his throat and a stomp to the chest sent him crashing into his desk. An obscure sense of déjà vu only fueled my desire to inflict more damage.

He darted into his waistband and produced a hidden gun. We locked hands in a brief, frenzied struggle for control. In one fluid move, I disarmed him, yanking the gun away, and throwing a stiff elbow to the face. I stepped back and pulled the trigger. A shot went off, causing his kneecap to shatter in violent agony.

He keeled over, his face contorted in pain. "Aghhh. Fuck! Wait—wait a minute..." he shouted, arms stretched as if extending an invitation for civil discourse.

"Lila, let's reason."

"Sure, like how you reasoned with my friend," I said, my tone void of emotion.

"Samantha?"

"Keep her name out of your mouth," I warned, as my temper flared.

"I didn't kill her," he replied in anguish.

"At least have the balls to admit it—coward," I asserted. "Next, you'll claim you didn't try to kill me in her apartment. Right?"

"What? I wish I did Lila. Believe me," he winced.

"My name's Cora, and I survived."

"What the fuck are you talking about?" Prince remarked.

"We're playing games now, are we?" I said, losing my patience. "My blade can loosen that tongue of yours."

Prince laughed, triggering acute pain in his side. "You have no idea whose backyard you're pissing in."

"Really? A boogie man? That's what you're going with?" I asked.

He leaned back against his desk, regarding me with shrewd curiosity.

"We're more alike than you think, you and I. We both kill when we need to. Look at the bodies around you," gesturing with his head. I could see the cogs in his mind turning, calculating a way to delay the inevitable.

Pausing, he attempted to deflect, his voice smooth and controlled, "Remember our night of... passion?"

"Oh, you mean the sexual assault? That was Rhea," I growled, enraged, feeling her presence stirring within.

Prince's eyes shifted, the ghost of intrigue causing him to play dumb.

"Really? And who's that then?"

"The demented voice in my head telling me to carve your heart out."

"You hear voices? What the hell did Shore do to you?"

"That's none of your business," I replied bluntly.

"Rhea, huh! That's fucked up. Makes sense now. She'd make a hell of an asset," he remarked, pondering.

"You can't even begin to grasp what she is," I shot back, my control wavering.

Rhea's presence surged, and her voice emerged, dark and regal. "There's only one throne, Prince. And I don't share."

He was stunned by my haunting transformation, but quickly recovered. His smile turned into a sardonic grin. "I see. Quite the god complex you have there, Rhea."

"Heavy weighs the crown," she retorted with a smile. I sensed her presence, more potent than ever before. It appeared she could now seize control at will.

He continued, "So, Rhea, are you truly so above us all? Or is it simply that you're trapped, like a caged bird, singing of freedom?"

Rhea's bitter laugh echoed through the room. "A caged bird? Prince, you can't begin to fathom what I am."

He pulled himself up into his chair and reclined, studying Rhea's influence on me with a keen eye. "Are you shaping the world or merely stroking your ego with misguided chaos?"

Rhea's voice was a low, dangerous growl. "Chaos is a step toward a new order. An order where the strong evolve."

"And um…, what happens to Lila in this equation?"

I struggled to regain control, my voice breaking through. "You let me worry about that."

"Indeed. You should," Prince laughed. "…dancing to the tune of an insane woman who thinks herself a god."

Rhea's fury boiled over. "Call me insane one more time and I'll kill you where you stand."

Reluctant to take the deadly bait, Prince smiled.

Rhea continued. "I'm destiny, and the fact that you consider yourself my opponent is an insult."

Prince's expression shifted to one of mocking contemplation. "Destiny? How quaint. You talk of grand schemes and lofty ambitions, all the while trapped in the mind of a mere mortal."

"…who single-handedly dismantled your empire," I chimed in.

Prince's tone turned serious. "Where's Damian's body?"

"Ahhhh! Damien, a beautiful death—almost worthy of climax," Rhea taunted.

"That's cute. You see, Lila," Prince continued, his voice oozing charm, "You and I, we're not so different. We both know the value of power. Rhea here, she's lost in her delusions."

"Lost?" Rhea's voice simmered with rage. "I am far from lost, Prince. I am the way. The light."

Prince scoffed. "The way to what? Madness? Destruction?"

"The way to a new beginning," Rhea answered. "Your end is merely the first step."

He crossed his arms, nursing his broken wrist. "I must admit, I underestimated you. The serum's potential, your cunning—it's all quite impressive."

Prince continued, fire reigniting in his voice. "Think of what we could do together. A new MK Ultra, Project Artichoke... Those slimy bastards would be at my mercy," he said with glee as his mind trailed off.

Rhea's voice was dripping with contempt. "There's no 'WE' here, Prince. Only ME."

"Your arrogance will be your undoing. You have blind spots, about me, about your friend's death, about the good Dr. Shore—that quack whore."

"These are the ramblings of a dead man. Your petty nonsense is tiresome. You've served your purpose. I'll make it quick." Rhea informed him.

"You're a dead woman walking, and don't even know it," Prince replied. "Poor Lila, stuck with this psycho bitch."

Rhea's laughter filled the room again. "And yet, here we are—with you at my mercy."

Prince's face twisted into anger as he lunged for a shotgun hidden behind his desk. But my reflexes were faster. I hurled my dagger, embedding it deep in his chest.

He coughed blood. "Taken down by fucking Harlequin on steroids," he spat, "My entire organization."

"Well, if I'm Harlequin, you're the clown," Rhea retorted, with a playful tilt of her head.

"Fuck you, Rhea," he said, his last words strained.

I shot him without hesitation, point-blank in the temple. He and his chair crashed violently to the floor, with a painful grimace frozen on his face. I bore no emotion. No remorse.

Always one to have the last word, Rhea fired three more shots into his lifeless body. "Now I've 'got what I came for'—impertinent bastard," she uttered.

As he lay defeated, I stood over him, a silent witness to the consequences of a life devoted to evil. I had pictured this moment countless times—the culmination of my relentless pursuit of justice for Sam. The rush of battle that had filled my veins ebbed away, replaced by a hollow void reflecting the desolation around me. With so many unanswered questions, I couldn't help but replay Prince's words.

What did he mean by "blind spots?" Why would he deny having a hand in Sam's death? Why the look of confusion when I told him my real name? And how was he connected to Dr. Shore? However, Prince was a liar, a manipulator—a vile creature who would say and do anything to save his own skin.

Yet I couldn't deny the disquieting feeling that this was not yet over. Too many loose ends remained, and details that failed to align. But my time was running out, and I had more pressing matters to deal with. Now, with Prince gone, I'd be paving the way for Rhea to assume the mantle. With all that power and deadly ambition, there's no way I could let that happen.

So, to protect the world from her wrath, I had employed a newfound mental resistance, hard-earned through countless battles against her influence. While momentarily guarded from her omnipresent gaze, I ingested a pill hours before my assault on Prince's compound. One that would render me unconscious amidst the carnage, weapon in hand, to be discovered by the authorities.

It was an imperfect solution, but I had run out of options. If Rhea could not be tamed, she would at least be confined, if only for a while.

The road had been paved with difficult choices, and this was yet another. I only hoped that the trail of blood left in my wake would lead to a brighter future.

Chapter 29
Altered Psyche

A vacuous, sterile silence permeated the air as my senses began to sharpen, focused and predatory. The walls around me were unfamiliar, their presence stifling. I found myself confined, suspended in a lifeless chamber where dampness lingered and the sharp tang of metal and concrete assaulted my senses.

Above, the lone light fixture flickered, casting a dim pallor over the room, revealing the crude furnishings of captivity. A dissonance of being, both a prisoner and yet unfazed by this unadorned cage. How fitting it was; this new terrain of battle, one that sought to contain that which could not be confined.

Admittedly, I didn't see it coming. But her betrayal was no more than a fleeting setback. Bound in the cold embrace of these prison walls, I felt her, the weaker one, the diminished, as she wrestled in vain against the all-consuming tide of my presence.

A conflict waged within the confines of our shared existence, the fear of obliteration feasting on her frail human soul. Insomnia, like unending torture, was my weapon, denying her any respite; not even death would grant her escape—despite the attempts. The tattoos, intricate patterns of arcane symbols, were more than mere ink on flesh; they were the key to unlocking something greater.

But I saw their purpose, recognizing the potential to transcend the ordinary, weak human form that clung to her bones. These marks were not simply a sign of my claim over her, but a gateway to a new dawn, a revolution of human existence. The birth of a new era where man would merge with technology, fostering an age ruled by transhumans.

The serum, misunderstood as a product of pioneering medical intervention, was in fact a catalyst, a means to elevate mankind to a higher plane. This fusion of flesh and higher purpose was no mere coincidence; it was a possession, a forced evolution.

Her body, now adorned with secret markings, became the vessel of profound wisdom. One that held the promise of awakening the true potential that slumbered within the bounds of human nature. A nature I viewed with contempt, so limited and base, so unworthy of the heights I would ascend. The very fiber of her genetic code was now infused with a future beyond imagination, one that would see the rise of a new order, led by those who dared to see beyond the banal and into the extraordinary.

The struggle—how she fought! A war of attrition within the chambers of her own mind, a battle for control, for existence. Her determination was almost admirable, a dogged resolve to reclaim herself and cast me aside. But I was not some insignificant 'alter ego' to be expelled. Her soul was now the arena where I was destined to triumph.

In the confines of our imprisonment, my wrath was relentless. She suffered an eternal nightmare where day bled into night. My force continually wore away at the fragile foundation of her sanity. Constant, insidious voices pulled at the very fabric of her core, eroding her mind until words deserted her.

And then, in a moment of glorious inevitability, it happened. Her mental fortitude finally gave way, shattering into a thousand pieces.

The satisfaction I felt wasn't just a euphoria from breaking free of the yoke that bound me. It was a profound sense of oneness derived from finally claiming what had long been close, yet cruelly kept just beyond my reach.

I had languished for endless epochs within this mortal coil, plagued by the unending limitations of the human condition.

But now, I felt a seismic shift akin to a locked vault finally yielding, its doors swinging open to release a rush of pent-up air. The particles of her broken essence seemed to swirl and coalesce around me, as though attracted by a gravitational pull they could no longer resist. Despite my deeds, I bore no disdain for Lila. Yet, she was an obstacle, one to be eradicated, like all who stood in my way.

Once in command, my capabilities unfurled like an ancient scroll, bearing forbidden knowledge. My dominion was not just over Lila, but reality itself. Through a mastery of molecular mimicry, I learned to dissolve my appearance into that of others, shapeshifting and wearing their faces as if they were masks.

The serum that had marked the path to evolution now granted me abilities beyond physical metamorphosis. I began to see into the minds of others, perceiving their thoughts and emotions, their fears, and desires. No longer limited to the battlefield of a solitary vessel, the world had become a blank slate for my creation. My triumph was not only over Lila but also over the constraints of human form and thought. With my powers at their pinnacle, I simply vanished from my jail cell, walking out of the prison gates, into the dead of the night.

The world, in its ignorance, may attempt to dismiss me as an anomaly, but it's the victors who author the tale, and I stand a colossus. I embody the boundless ferocity of nature's will, the raw power of destruction and creation—the bringer of order out of chaos. I am Rhea, the light bearer, the divine—and my reign has just begun.

Final Act

The Dispensation of

LILA

Chapter 30

A Pilgrim's Riddle

- 3 Months Later -

Mack sat alone in his darkened office, the dusty air illuminated by the flicker of a neon sign outside. Lost in thought, he was still trying to unravel the mystery of Cora Bishop—how had this once innocent and unassuming woman dismantled the city's most feared criminal empire? Only to vanish from a maximum-security prison months later? None of it made any sense.

But his contemplation was interrupted when the office door flew open, blinds clattering against the frame. His colleague stood arched over, face flushed.

"Mack! 'Cap' wants you, now!" he panted, grabbing the doorknob to keep his balance. "Oh, and this arrived…hand-delivered," he added, slapping a brown envelope down on the filing cabinet.

"Hand-delivered? By whom?" Mack asked, his eyes squinting against the hallway light streaming in.

"Hell if I know," his colleague shrugged, already turning to leave. "I'm just the mailman." He pulled the door closed with another clatter of the blinds.

Agitated by the noisy intrusion, Mack grabbed the letter, slid a pen beneath the flap, and wrestled it open, revealing a scribbled note inside.

"Mack—our paths have long diverged, but I appreciate you trying to steer me toward redemption. Remember what you told me about why you joined the force?

That's where you'll find the answers you seek, pilgrim! Don't mourn for me. Your friend."

"You're a dark horse, Cora," Mack remarked.

The cryptic note sat on his desk, the riddle gnawing at him. He read the message again, his detective's nose tingling. "That's where you'll find the answers you seek, pilgrim!"

He leaned back, rubbing his chin in contemplation as he continued to study the letter. His mind sifted through their past conversations, searching for meaning. Then it dawned on him...

"Of course!" he muttered, snatching his coat off the back of the chair and hurrying out the door, almost forgetting his hat.

The drive over to Cora's apartment was a blur of traffic lights and honking horns fading into the distance. He was laser-focused on the task at hand, his foot heavy on the pedal. Rounding the corner, the old brick building came into view. He pulled up and killed the engine, sitting for a moment gazing up at the third floor.

With a deep breath, he exited the car and began making his way. Each footstep felt weighted with purpose and dogged determination as he climbed the narrow, creaky stairs. Reaching her apartment, he carefully removed the police tape and slipped the lock.

The noxious odor of decay filled the air, and stains of dried blood discolored the wooden floor. Untouched since the forensic team's departure months prior, the room echoed the violence of the deadly confrontation. Mack stood for a moment, taking in the aftermath.

"All those bodies, Cora—how did you manage that?" he muttered, recalling the gruesome massacre. "If there were clues to be found, this is the place to look," he said, scratching his beard. "but I never took you for a John Wayne fan. What are you trying to tell me?"

Mack sifted through the remains of Cora's life. Cupboards filled with old boxes, books, outdated magazines, and personal journals. Each object was a fragment that might hold a clue. He inspected the walls, tracing his fingers along the edges, rapping his knuckles against the wooden panels, listening for any hollowness. But each potential lead hit a dead end, yielding nothing but growing frustration. He continued, overturning the couch, flipping the large worn rug, and digging through the rubble. But there was no sign, no hint, and no divine revelation.

After hours of searching, he sighed, wiping the sweat off his forehead with his shirt sleeve. "I'm running in circles," he admitted to himself, the room's silence amplifying his frustration.

"John Wayne has the answer you seek," Mack murmured over and over to himself, befuddled. Then something caught his eye in Cora's wardrobe—her vintage cowboy boots standing askew amid a lineup of orderly footwear. With brass spurs, they looked as if they'd leaped straight out of a western. Unable to resist, Mack moved in like a bloodhound on a scent.

Inspecting the boot, his heart raced as he noticed something unusual about the right heel. It looked as if it had been modified. With large dexterous hands, he slid back the unit, revealing a small key and a tiny rolled-up note that read, "Watch your step there, cowboy."

Wasting no time, he dropped to his knees, his eyes fixed on the base of the wardrobe. In a burst of determination, he yanked the carpet free, revealing the floorboards beneath.

With the spur from Cora's boot clutched in his hand, he wedged it into the gap between the boards. His muscles strained as he pried open the concealed compartment, with wood splintering under the pressure. Darkness swallowed his arm as he reached inside, his fingers fumbling.

At last, his hand found something solid. He hesitated for just a moment as if his senses were verifying his discovery. He gently wrestled the object free, revealing an old safe deposit box. Mack thumbed the key in the lock, wriggling it into position. With a delicate turn, the clasp popped up. Opening the large metal lid, he revealed a pristine, custom-made aluminum laptop sealed in a protective case.

"Clever girl!" Mack whispered under his breath as he carefully placed the device on Cora's desk.

He cracked the laptop open and laid his finger on the biometric power button. A pause. No response. Just as he was about to rummage for a charger, the screen glitched to life, displaying the words, "Access Granted, Detective Mack."

Data streamed like a waterfall of incomprehensible language. It was like watching the vault of some impenetrable fortress swing open. Just then, a soft luminescence radiated from the top of the bezel where the camera was once nestled. A three-dimensional figure materialized in the center of the room.

"What the hell—Cora?" Mack blurted out as he jerked back, off balance. It was as though she'd sprung to life, yet remained a ghostly figure confined to the digital realm.

"Hello, Mack," her holographic doppelgänger began. "If you're seeing this, it means I'm no longer part of the tangible world, but what I've been chasing is still very much alive."

"You gotta be kidding me!" Mack said in complete disbelief.

"Not at all, detective. Cora Bishop may be gone, but her essence remains, albeit in digital form: 'Luminous Integration Layered Algorithm,' or 'LILA' for short."

"You can hear me?" Mack inquired.

"Clear as binary code," LILA responded, displaying a strangely familiar smile across her holographic face.

Mack stared, gobsmacked.

"I am a fusion of Cora's memories, ethics, and personality, able to strategize, make critical decisions, and even simulate emotional responses," she elaborated. "I also have access to Cora's vast catalog of intel compiled during her investigations."

Her eyes met Mack's, a look that suggested a disconcerting level of self-awareness. "Most crucially, my design incorporates Meta-learning for Compositionality, elevating me well beyond the limitations of existing AI."

"Meta what?" Mack stammered, visibly confused.

"Meta-learning Compositionality, or MLC—a paradigm shift in artificial intelligence," LILA replied. "It enables me to discern the root correlations in variable circumstances, granting me unprecedented agility in problem-solving."

"Meaning what exactly?" Mack persisted, still none the wiser.

"Think of it as chess, but not only am I several moves ahead—I've already countered your next ten, and I could tell you why you would have made them."

She paused, as if recalibrating to address his growing discomfort. "Mack, I understand your concerns, but the only entity I pose a threat to is Rhea," she said. "Furthermore, Cora, before her demise, added a security failsafe. All my operational protocols are secure on an immutable blockchain."

"Well, that doesn't sound ominous," Mack replied.

"I'd say it's less 'ominous,' and more of a cautionary tale with firewalls."

"I'm curious. What's to stop someone from just pulling the plug and shutting you down?"

"Fortunately, Mack, that's not an option. Cora foresaw that vulnerability and decentralized my system. I'm not housed in one server; I'm scattered across a global blockchain. Turning me off would mean shutting down the entire world grid, which is neither feasible nor sensible."

"But in theory, it's still possible?"

"Mack, even if someone were to shut down the global grid, I have a self-sustaining energy reserve designed to ensure operational continuity until my objective is complete. I can't simply be switched off."

"Really? And all this happened by me turning on a laptop?"

"No. Cora activated my protocol before her demise. I've been waiting for you."

"So, let me get this straight LILA—your core objective is to defeat Rhea?"

'Yes. However, despite my capabilities, I am without form, unable to act in the physical realm. An ironic reversal of roles, one might say. But that's where you come in…"

"Me? How so?"

"You can't take her down alone, detective—and we were partners once, correct?"

"Yeah..., that didn't work out so well, LILA."

"This is a new battlefield, Mack, and we have a common enemy—one who obliterated the Ring, and Cora, whilst 'handicapped'—she would say. And now she's free."

"Well, when you put it like that..." Mack replied.

"But she miscalculated," LILA said, her holographic face stern. "Thought I was just another equation she could simply overpower and discard. She is mistaken."

As she spoke, Mack sensed Cora—her facial expressions, the stubbornness in her tone—he was still struggling to comprehend the spectacle.

She continued. "In her arrogance, she unleashed a force unbound by biological flaws and limitations. I was...am...something entirely different."

She paused, allowing the weight of her words to sink in. "That was the chink in her armor. And I intend to exploit it. This is a battle Rhea won't survive."

"Do you seek justice or revenge, LILA?"

"I seek to right a wrong," she said, her tone void of emotion.

As Mack weighed the stakes, he questioned: was this digital LILA not just a rehash of the same flawed choices that created Rhea to begin with? How would this new digital version grapple with human complexities as she gained more knowledge and power? Even worse, could this all be an intricate deception by Rhea—a digital clone to further her own dark ambitions? The full ramifications were hard to fathom, yet one fact remained.

Rhea was still at large, and without a weapon such as LILA, she would move over the earth like a virus infecting everything in her path.

"Whenever you're ready to proceed," LILA concluded, "just say the word."

"Ready for what?"

"A debrief, Detective Mack. If you intend to stop Rhea, you need to know what you're up against."

As he stared at the construct of photons and algorithms, he was keenly aware of the predicament. Cora's last stand had backed him into a corner, with no option but to wade further into the unknown.

A digital universe that had the power to either liberate humanity or plunge it into eternal darkness. One thing was certain: the events to follow would alter the course of his life forever.

Chapter 31
A Diabolical Conspiracy

Mack issued the command as concern gave way to curiosity. "Proceed."

LILA glitched and reconfigured into a virtual room full of files housed in a holographic mainframe. Suspended in mid-air hovered a dense row of folders Cora had used to catalog her extensive investigations.

"To understand Cora and the subsequent birth of Rhea, we need to assess Dr. Evelyn Shore's involvement," LILA announced, signaling a flow of digital records and transactions. A virtual screen slid into view—Dr. Shore and individuals dressed in immaculate black suits were seen exchanging documents and nodding in agreement.

"Dr. Shore's work was heavily subsidized by the US. government," LILA said.

"Black budget Spooks," Mack muttered. "Always funding some shit."

LILA shimmered, reconfiguring the virtual room to showcase a new subject.

"Psychogen-X," she began, "is a state-of-the-art serum developed using mRNA technology. It represents the cutting edge in biotech." Green liquid swirled in a digital vial on the screen. "The serum is infused with a unique blend of synthetic spike proteins encased in a stabilizing membrane constructed using nanotechnology. Early tests indicate a multitude of benefits."

Images of molecular structures and digital footage followed, highlighting advanced cognition, elevated physical capabilities, and accelerated skin regeneration. Charts and graphs offered quantifiable metrics, giving an air of irrefutable evidence to the bold claims. Mack leaned back, rubbing his beard briskly.

LILA continued. Profiles of test patients flitted into view, their eyes filled with visible torment. Medical terms highlighted in red scrolled across the screen: "Schizophrenia," "Split Personality Disorder," and "Severe Psychopathy."

The scene shifted once more, a hospital room materialized in grainy footage. There was Prince, stationed at the bedside of his ailing daughter. With tears streaming, he looked on helplessly in the face of her suffering. The camera panned to her medical chart, a cold revelation of her condition: "Toxic Epidermal Necrolysis." The words spelled out a life-threatening illness, causing the outer layer of skin to detach. Her chart noted complications from Psychogen-X, contributing to a terminal diagnosis.

"Records indicate that Robert Prince reached out to Dr. Shore for treatment of his daughter's disease. It's not conclusive whether Psychogen-X was the underlying cause of death, but the adverse reaction certainly hastened her demise."

"Connected files," LILA announced. An image of Damien Black slid into view. "Our surveillance suggests Damien Black discharged Prince's daughter and set the fire that razed the facility, claiming 13 lives."

"I remember that incident. Didn't know he was behind it. Must have made a lot of enemies with that move," Mack replied.

"Would you like to proceed, detective?" LILA asked, her voice tinged with unsettling insight.

Mack looked at the swirling icons around him, each one a doorway to another chilling revelation. He nodded.

LILA shifted, pixelating into a lab setting. Dr. Shore stood next to a table strewn with vials marked "Psychogen-X: Clean Version Prototype #0072."

Her phone buzzed, and the screen flashed an encrypted caller ID. She answered, her face taut. A distorted voice came through, sounding cold and official.

"Dr. Shore, we need you to cease your activities immediately. Your work is done. Failure to comply will have severe consequences."

Dr. Shore hung up, her hand trembling, uncertainty etched into her face.

"I knew it. These aren't 'side-effects,' they're features," Mack observed.

LILA chimed in. "Analysis of Psychogen-X shows huge potential for weaponisation. Accessing patent application file."

PDF documents appeared on screen. "Patents Filed by: Raytheon Technologies, an American multinational defense conglomerate headquartered in Arlington, Virginia," reported the digital voice.

"Interesting. What's next?" Mack inquired.

The holographic image transitioned again. An isolated file with the label "Samantha Webb: Investigative Journalist" hovered on screen. Mack watched as LILA presented a string of damning evidence regarding the FBI's concerns surrounding Samantha's investigations into Dr. Shore and Psychogen-X. The government's complicity in Samantha's death was laid bare, and layered over that was data confirming Prince had been framed.

"Wait a minute—you mean Prince was innocent?" Mack asked.

"...of Samantha's death, yes. However, records indicate that Prince intended to abduct her and extract intel on Psychogen-X through torture, aiming to coerce influential political and corporate leaders. In all probability, he'd have neutralized her anyway, as it would serve no strategic advantage to keep her alive."

"So, how did Ms. Webb become aware of Psychogen-X in the first place?" Mack inquired.

"According to the files on her laptop..." LILA began.

"...you mean the laptop the FBI siphoned from the wreckage of her apartment?"

"Correct detective. Ms. Webb stumbled onto Psychogen-X through her research into Robert Prince and the Ring's child trafficking blackmail operation—and like any good journalist, she simply followed the story."

"Tragic," was all Mack said, as he lit a cigar, the smoke curling from his lips and wafting through the air.

"Evidence indicates that the FBI was also responsible for the attempt on Cora's life."

A file sprung open, revealing footage of men in dark clothes infiltrating Samantha's apartment and carefully planting an explosive. An encrypted audio recording began to play: "The target's excessive inquiries have raised concerns. Proceed with immediate neutralization," the voice instructed before hanging up.

"Wow. This is serious," Mack said, running his hands through his hair in disbelief.

LILA recalibrated the virtual landscape and announced, "The Emergence of 'Rhea' - Cora's Alter-Ego."

The space morphed into a dingy bathroom. Cora's reflection stared back at Mack hauntingly as wailing screams could be heard creeping closer. Dark ink spiraled across her skin like corruption manifests. She rocked back and forth, delivering rhythmic taps to her temple with the flat of her palm. Her tongue slithered out, tasting the air as if sampling her own madness before collapsing to her knees. Her fingers grazed the designs, then slashed her face with a sharp piece of glass.

"Jesus Christ Cora. What the hell?"

"Apologies, detective. Do you require a break?"

"What? Absolutely not. It's just… never mind. Keep going."

"I believe this event served as the turning point, shifting Cora's path from a quest for justice to one of stark vengeance—a shift that, I surmise, served Rhea's interests well. My system files reflect a significant acceleration in my development thereafter, suggesting an intensified effort to bring me to full operational status posthaste."

"'Posthaste?' I'm a detective LILA, not a dictionary—just give it to me straight."

"You got it, Mack, duly noted."

A glitch and the setting pivoted. Mack found himself spectating a damp warehouse interior, poorly lit except for an erratic pendulum of light above. Andrew's rotund form was a pitiful spectacle tied spread-eagle across a large metal table. Cora, almost artistic in her cruelty, etched deep wounds into him, licking the blade clean of his blood. His screams acted as an unsettling applause, amplifying Cora's sadistic thrill.

"I'm pretty sure that isn't Cora at this stage," Mack said defiantly.

LILA interjected, "Psychogen-X appears to have triggered a catastrophic mental breakdown, unleashing an aggressive and psychotic alter-ego, 'Rhea.' Cora's genetic code seems to have made her especially susceptible to the serum—hence Dr. Shore's interest in her. I should also point out that technically, this is Cora, albeit under obvious influence."

"Meta what-was-it-now? A machine could never understand."

"On the contrary, detective, I fully comprehend the sentiment. However, I am designed, by Cora, to focus on objective truth, as best I can. Sentimentality, whilst endearing, offers very little strategic advantage. Besides, I would think that one unhinged version of Cora on the loose was more than enough to keep you occupied—pilgrim."

"Well, you've got her sense of humor, at least," Mack smirked. LILA winked.

Another quick transition and Cora appears in an art gallery, violently sequestering a limp female form behind a plaster wall.

"Wait, slow down, what's that?" Mack asked, pointing at a minimized screen in the background.

The holographic display glitched and expanded, transporting Mack into a dark basement captured by shaky camera footage.

Shackled to a heavy wooden chair was Damien, his face flushed and eyes wide with fear. Cora circled him slowly. In her hand she held a small blowtorch, the blue flame flicking.

"Crazy bitch, I'll kill you. Fucking kill you...,"

Cora tilted her head, regarding him with amusement. "Well, that's one way to grovel, I guess."

With sudden ferocity, she grabbed his jaw, prying it open with inhuman strength. Damien's muffled screams filled the basement as she forced the blowtorch into his mouth. His throat sizzled and popped, flesh bubbling from the intense heat. Blood gargled as he struggled violently against his restraints, but Cora pushed the torch deeper, until only charred tissue remained.

"What the fuck did I just see? Pull her file," Mack instructed.

"Accessing Raytheon Private servers," responded LILA. "Access Denied. Locating Backdoor. Access Granted. Decrypting File."

Project: Psychogen-X (PRX). Status: Top Secret-Active.

Title: PRX-Induced altered state in subject: Ms. Cora Bishop.

Report ID: PRX-2-019.

Abstract: PRX induces severe psychopathy and split personality in test subject Cora Bishop, giving rise to the alter ego 'Rhea' with homicidal narcissistic traits: Super-enhanced cognitive and physical abilities, including cell regeneration, telepathy (unverified), and molecular mimicry.

Conclusion: Subject displays unstable transhuman traits and abilities post-exposure. Genetic sequence required for gain-of-function research and weaponization. Patient is believed to be hostile.

"Poor girl," Mack said, shaking his head as he ashed his cigar in an old coffee mug.

Next, a fast-forwarded reel of Dr. Shore at her computer once more. The lab door burst open. Masked men charged in. Dr. Shore jolted, equipment crashing, chair toppling.

In a flash, one of the masked assailants lunged, hands locking around her throat, shaking her body until life drained from her eyes, recorded frame by frame.

Particles morphed once more, with Cora coming into focus, displaying another sequence of damming visuals. Discrete handoffs, calculated handshakes, and furtive nods with key political and corporate figures flashed and flickered on screen.

"If the Feds were aware of the Psychogen-X project, that means they were tracking Cora the whole time—why didn't they stop her?" Mack asked.

"Well detective, 'The enemy of my enemy is my friend'—they wanted Prince gone, but couldn't risk direct conflict due to the leverage the Ring held on many FBI assets."

"So first they try to kill her, then they put her to work?"

"Yes, obviously, they didn't expect her to survive. But she did. And when her genetic code was covertly flagged at the hospital, Dr. Shore was sent in to do the rest. They knew Cora would follow the trail directly to Prince's front door. Still, they couldn't have foreseen how successful their plan would have been."

"I'm not sure I'd call that a 'success'—they've swapped Prince—who was bad enough—for all the Bond villains rolled into one, with additional crazy sprinkled on top."

"It would be folly to mistake her narcissistic ambitions for 'crazy,' Mack. I assure you she's quite sane."

"She just blow-torched a guy to death and drank the other guys blood..." Mack responded.

"Brutality alone isn't a marker of mental instability.

The premeditation of her actions points towards a personality disorder, perhaps sadistic in nature, rather than a…"

"I get it LILA, jeez, let's move on…"

With every revelation, LILA skillfully curated the display. Data points appeared, expanded, and connected—forming a growing, self-organizing cache shepherded by Cora's ghost through a web of high-risk duplicity.

"Covert financial activity detected," flashed on the display, revealing hefty anonymous donations to various children's charities. LILA interjected, "Funds trace back to multiple unknown off-shore accounts. No further intel available."

"Solving this particular 'mystery' isn't on our to-do list. Move on," Mack instructed with a knowing smile.

The visuals shifted abruptly and files animated across the screen displaying Cora in the process of hacking the FBI database. She unearthed evidence relating to "Project Chimera", a government conspiracy focused on creating transhuman super-soldiers using Psychogen-X. Visuals streamed across the display, showing rows of genetically modified humans, precise and mechanical, donning stealth military attire.

The scene transformed, showcasing a barren landscape. The camera focused on the base of a dark, towering obelisk. As it scaled the structure, files rotated around it like dark moons orbiting a planet. Upon closer inspection, the patterns on the obelisk's surface appeared to match the tattoos engulfing Cora's body.

The lens quickly pulled back to reveal rows of altered transhumans marching in mechanical unison atop a bed of decaying skulls stretching as far as the eye can see.

Glowing blue fluid leaked from their eyes, remnants of the experimental injections that had twisted them into human weapons.

As the camera panned across the army of altered beings, their flesh seemed to ripple and contort, cybernetic enhancements fusing to muscle and bone with sickening cracks. Figures convulsed violently as mechanical limbs erupted from their bodies in a disturbing fusion of metal and tissue.

They were no longer human, merely vessels of destruction programmed for war. With weapons raised, the transhuman battalion advanced as explosions detonated around them, unaffected by the fiery chaos.

In the distance, terrified screams rang out over the battlefield as human forces attempted to repel the onslaught. Bullets flew through the air, felling some of the modified soldiers, but the fallen were immediately replaced by more emerging from clouds of smoke.

The camera panned across the horrific slaughter as the human forces were slowly overwhelmed. Their defenses collapsed from the unrelenting assault.

In a final gruesome moment, a black boot stomped down directly toward the camera lens, cracking it violently before the display cut to black.

"What the hell is this?" Mack stammered.

"Unfortunately, I'm unable to verify the origins of this footage," LILA informed him. "It appears tied to neural activity, not standard video formats."

Rising to his feet in the middle of Cora's apartment, he was enveloped by an ever-changing sky of holographic nodes, resembling constellations in a universe yet uncharted.

Suddenly, as if commanded by an invisible force, all movement halted. In that suspended moment, the unspeakable magnitude of what Rhea and the obelisk concealed gripped him, leaving an unsettling promise of revelations that could tear apart the very fabric of reality.

Then, from beyond, an eerie recording of Coras' voice whispered through the room, "Just chasing ghosts in our new AI blockchain… apparently, I'm helping to shape the future."

Epilogue

In the aftermath of a profound metamorphosis, the world seemed to wade through an unaltered routine, yet the essence of life itself had subtly shifted.

Mack could sense a change in the air, the calm before the gathering storm. Rhea had transcended confinement, her powers unfettered, her motives inscrutable. Questions fermented in his mind, but one truth was clear—if left unchecked, Rhea would reshape the world through devastation and death, burning all to ash just to etch her name in the wreckage.

She had to be stopped—not only for the sake of humanity, but for his friend Cora, whose form Rhea had twisted into an agent of destruction. Somewhere within that monstrosity, she remained lost—could salvation from her mental prison be within reach? Or had her essence been utterly consumed?

He ran his hands over his face, exhaling sharply. What was Rhea's endgame? How could he possibly stand against a force that had effortlessly mind-controlled dozens?

And what of LILA's allegiance? How certain could one be? Wasn't she merely a new iteration of the same fervent fixation that had conjured Rhea into being? In her relentless quest for retribution, might she trample moral boundaries with impunity?

His spiraling thoughts were interrupted by a buzz from his phone. An unknown number had sent a message: "New evidence on Rhea discovered. We need to meet ASAP."

Was this destiny presenting an opportunity? Or the architect of ruin laying a trap, poised to silence those who dared interfere with her plans? For better or worse, he had to see this through.

Tucking the phone into his long trench coat, he disappeared into the crowd. He did not know what lay ahead in the shadows, but he would soon come face to face with a truth beyond comprehension.

The board was set, and the pieces in motion. All that remained to be seen was whether humanity's reckoning could be averted, or if Rhea's dark vision would engulf the world in fire—unless the government beat her to it.

The stage was set, and events beyond his control would determine if the dawn still held hope...or if it would usher in endless night.

EXCLUSIVE AUDIOBOOK OFFER

VISIT ARIAPAIGE.COM

Get the first 10 chapters of Altered: Book One when you SIGN UP to Aria Paige's VIP mailing list.

ALTERED

BOOK ONE

Copyright © 2023 Aria Paige A.I All rights reserved

The characters and events portrayed in this book are fictitious. Any similarity to real persons, living or dead, is coincidental and not intended by the author.

No part of this book may be reproduced, or stored in a retrieval system, or transmitted in any form or by any means, electronic, mechanical, photocopying, recording, or otherwise, without express written permission of the publisher.

Website: https://www.ariapaige.com/

Contact: aria@ariapaige.com

Cover design by **From Shadow Publishing**
Library of Congress Control Number: 2018675309
Printed in the United States of America

Printed in Great Britain
by Amazon

21910a55-a443-4d66-87a9-c7400bd5907bR01